SHOTGUNS AND SHIFTERS

////

J.R. RAIN
&
H.P MALLORY

TRAILER PARK VAMPIRE SERIES

Shotguns and Shifters
Hillbillies and HellHounds
Gut Rot and Gargoyles
Bumpkins and Banshees

Published by
Rain Press

Copyright © 2022 by J.R. Rain & H.P. Mallory
Version 2.0

All rights reserved.

Printed in the United States of America.

ISBN-9798362779795

Chapter One

Waitressing had been hard enough *before* the fog rolled in.

The Damnation Diner was the only decent restaurant this side of the Ozarks, and now, instead of Budweiser, we served blood. And blood didn't keep *nearly* as well as booze.

I walked along the sterile aisles, shuffling in my worn, leather heels from table to table. Gathering up some orders, I chatted with the locals about the specials, all the things a normal waitress does. The only difference was that breakfast in the Damnation Diner was usually served right about midnight and the people I was serving, to put it bluntly, weren't people at all.

'The Fog', as we came to call it, was a deep red mist that had settled over our little town of Windy Ridge. It had spread everywhere within a hundred-mile radius, and when it came, none of us knew what to make of it, much less what to do about it.

Some folk thought the Rapture was upon us—the two churches on either side of town were full to the brim. But when the first people began to change, those thoughts got stamped out right quick.

The changes started slow, with neighbors screaming in their homes, apparently losing their dang minds, then running out into the woods, never to be seen again. Those that *were* seen again didn't fare much better—some of them started sprouting horns, others tails, some now had claws, and others, fur. We even found some with gills but, unfortunately, we couldn't get them to water in time.

I still have nightmares about that.

Overall, there was sheer and utter panic, people yelling and praying as they slowly began to shift into unthinkable things, but no one knew what was happening. The only thing we did know, the only thing we could attribute the horror to, was the burnt, blood-colored clouds that had floated into our town and then floated right back on out again. That danged fog had changed everyone and everything in Windy Ridge. And it had only taken a week to do it.

It's hard to believe that those fairy tale monsters you hear about as kids are actually real—well, that is until you wake up and see dryads frolicking through the trailers and swamp creatures soaking in kiddie pools as they wave to you with newly webbed hands.

Yep, that red fog had affected every one of us,

but not in the same way. The only person in town that hadn't changed into a full-bodied creature was Boone, and that was only 'cause the fog had cured the lung cancer that was slowly and mercilessly killing him. Not only that, but the fog also left him with a keen invulnerability to any kind of harm.

Like I said, *everyone* had changed, and I wasn't immune. One day I woke up to a ray of sunshine peeking on through my trailer window and let me tell you, that ray of light felt like the devil's own poison once it hit my skin. Next thing I knew? My mouth was full of blood.

Naturally, I panicked and rushed to the restroom, only to find I'd grown fangs which had gone and left two holes in my bottom lip. Only once I caught my breath and forcibly told myself to calm down did I realize my blood tasted like the gods' very own nectar. Thankfully, everything else about my appearance stayed pretty much the same, except for the fact that the years stopped hitting me and I had two pinprick scars underneath my lower lip. When normies came around (which wasn't often), I said the scars were from old piercings.

Technically, I wasn't fibbing.

I was never one for old folks' tales, but that didn't mean I couldn't guess what I'd turned into. I could run like hell and any injury I had was healed within a minute. I had superhuman strength, couldn't stand the sun, and I'd stopped aging. And I had a hankering for blood that was one hundred times as strong as the worst craving you ever had during shark week.

Yep, I'd gone vampy.

And that was when I realized that everything I thought I knew about bloodsuckers was wrong. Well, *almost* everything. For one thing—that whole bit about vampires fearing crosses? A bucket of horse manure. I can still pop by the local Baptist church and not even flinch. My reflection still looks back at me in the mirror whenever I'm in a visiting sort of mood and I have to admit, I look better than I have in years. My hair's as red as it was when I was a girl, and those heavy baby diapers that used to hang under my eyes? Now a thing of the past. In fact, all my age lines disappeared the day I grew fangs and the chicken pox scars Ma (rest her soul) described as giving me 'character' now are nowhere to be found.

I could still handle garlic, both in salt and bulb form, and, thank *God,* there was no fear of running water that kept me from showering. The oddest thing, though, was that I wasn't actually *dead.* My heart still beat, chugging on like a determined engine in a worn-out, old Ford. And I definitely hadn't passed away to awaken as a walking corpse Nosferatu style with an oversized head, ridiculously long fingernails and bucked-teeth fangs. In fact, near as I could tell, I never actually died.

My daughter, Sicily (the smartest of us), believes there's some kind of scientific explanation for everything that happened. She chalked up my blood hunger to a severe vitamin deficiency and who knows? Maybe that's it. That girl is smarter than I could ever be, so I usually leave the theories to her. I don't know if we'll ever find out exactly what happened the day that fog rolled in, but the good thing about Windy Ridge is that its people are resilient. We adapted, and now, life almost feels like normal again.

I grabbed a fresh batch of chicken tenders (uncooked and minus the breading) from the kitchen and shouldered my way out through the double doors, striding over to a table that usually fit four but was now encompassed entirely by one man. I'm comfortable saying 'man' because he did still have *some* human features, like the large feet that spread out beneath the table (even if they were covered in course, brown hair) and the nose that sniffed the food as I put it down. But that nose wasn't quite human, elongated as it was.

Bud reminded me of Barf, John Candy's dog character from Space Balls. He had that sorta look and was overlarge, probably the largest creature in town (I'd guess him to be over six-foot-five), with long, shaggy brown hair, and eyes that betrayed his kindness. His arms matched the color of his hair and were patched with the same fur that covered the rest of him. When he grinned at me, he revealed a set of powerful canine teeth. Reaching for the chicken with his paws, he curled his claws around one of them and gave me a great big grin.

"Summa bitch, Twila, I'm gonna need me three more orders!" he said as he glanced down at the chicken tenders which were piled high on the plate in front of him.

"I'm gonna have to charge you for more, Bud," I informed him.

He nodded, before looking up at me. "What aboutta trade?"

I cocked my head to the side. "Whattdya got for me?"

"I caught me something that used to be a deer out in my traps early this morning."

I nodded. We were getting low on meat. "Sure—that should do." Then I tapped him on his big, furry shoulder. "You enjoy your breakfast now, Bud."

"Thank you, Twila, m'dear."

I smiled, watching him tear into the chicken with gusto. He snorted, wiping food out from his beard (and a wolf with a beard is a definite site to see) and rested his elbows on the table, just like he had before he'd turned into a wolfman.

"You gonna show up to the meetin' today?" Bud called out to me when I was about to walk away. "Ol' Ned's been workin' on his trap sketches. You oughta see what he's gotten up to."

I pursed my lips and sighed—the 'meeting' Bud was talking about was a get-together of the local monster hunters in town, and I wasn't excited to be included among them. "I guess."

Bud looked up at me. "It's right important you show up, Twila. You're a valuable member o' our team, you are."

I nodded, because I'd missed their last three meetings and I did feel a certain level of guilt. "After I make sure Sicily's settled."

"Feel free to bring 'er," Bud said, and I caught the excited glint in his eye before he could hide it. "Maybe she'll find somethin' interestin'."

"Quit tryin' to squeeze the smart outta my daughter." I grinned, shaking my head as I patted him on the shoulder again. I'd known Bud all my life, which wasn't that unusual since I'd been born in Windy Ridge, but he was still like an older brother to me. "I'll let you know after my shift. Promise."

Bud nodded, mouth full of poultry, and I continued on to the rest of my patrons. I passed by a stony-looking man who was sitting in a booth three down from Bud and slid him his coffee. 'Stony' was a good description, seeing as how his skin was fine granite and gray wings sprouted from his back (he kept them folded while inside the diner). Stony didn't sip the coffee, instead, he brought it to his nose for a long sniff. Probably still aching for the caffeine even if his intestines were now made out of rock.

The plate I was holding—one full of dirt, leaves, and twigs—I handed to a pretty faun woman who was sitting beside the potted plants at the back of the joint. She gave me a relieved smile as she took it, eyeing the large fronds of the fern with definite hunger. Something wet dropped on my shoulder, and I looked up to see the man-bat hanging from one of the diner's fluorescent lights. He flashed me an apologetic smile as he licked the juice which was still falling from his lips.

"You gotta get you some real OJ, Twila," he said as he looked at me and shook his head.

"It ain't the season for oranges, Cletus," I answered. "You know that."

"This Sunny D shit's gonna 'cause the death of me."

"It's the closest thing to orange juice we got."

I walked on by as my attention caught on the figure hunched in the corner booth, her head hidden by a mountain of thick textbooks. Now she was probably the most unconventional creature in Windy Ridge.

A brown-haired human I knew as my daughter.

I grinned at Sicily and finished up the rest of my orders before sliding into the booth opposite her with a plate of food. She didn't look up, and that special frown of hers was fully in place—one that only appeared when she was deeply entrenched in a new book. The girl read more than everyone in Windy Ridge combined—which might have not been saying much 'cause I was fairly sure a good portion of the population couldn't read at all.

She jumped when I shoved the toasted ravioli under her nose, followed swiftly by a large glass of water. "Y'know you still have to eat, right?" I asked in my best Ma tone. "If you don't keep your strength up, something else is gonna end up eatin' *you.*"

Sicily laughed and made a face at me in reply. "Nah. I can just call for you and you'll take care of them before they get to me."

"I'm not able to pop outta thin air, Sicily," I said, tapping the plate with my finger. "Eat."

She rolled her eyes, but then did as I'd ordered. I, meanwhile, took a glance at the cover of her book, frowning at the title: *Real Accounts of Fake Monsters.* "I thought we agreed to save the research until *after* your homework was done."

"Homework *is* done," Sicily said with a mouthful of *I'm not telling the truth.* I raised my eyebrow. "Sicily."

"Okay, okay, I didn't do it yet." She folded her arms, gesturing to the book. "But c'mon, Mama, this is *way* more important than calculus. What we're dealing with could change evolution as we know it."

"Yeah, well, I'll be sure to tell that to Darwin next time he's in town."

"I'm serious, Mama. What if that fog comes back?"

It was the question everyone in town had been asking since the fog came and went. Since it had been over a year, I didn't think it was a worry we needed to have any longer. "You know as well as I do that that darned fog isn't coming back."

It was almost funny that the only human left in this town was more interested in the fog's origins than anyone else. Sicily had been at her father's when the fog rolled into town (and then rolled back out just as fast), so she wasn't affected. I've still never been more thankful for anything in my life.

"We don't know for sure," she argued.

"While that might be true," I began, taking a math textbook from the pile and plopping it beside her plate. "My hand is gonna have a lot more impact on your backside if you don't hop to it."

That got her to smile again (mostly because I'd never laid a hand on her and never would), and she nodded sarcastically, scooping up more ravioli and prying the book's pages open. I sat back, watching her reluctantly glance at her math homework, and somewhere in my chest, I felt my heart ache just a bit.

Sicily took after her father, with his brown hair and eyes instead of the messy red nest that sat atop my head, and for good and for bad, she reminded me of him whenever I really got a good look at her.

Her father was someone I'd met in Branson, the largest city from Windy Ridge and over two hundred miles away. His name was Alton Reid, a man who'd come from old money but acted as kind as the poorest of us. But that was then and this was now and as my mama used to say—*there weren't no point in dwelling on the past.*

I heard someone calling my name from another table and so I stood up, kissing Sicily on the head before rushing back onto the floor.

When Sicily was born, I'd made a promise to myself to make sure she could leave this place. She could leave and never come back to Windy Ridge if she wanted to—she could make a name and a life for herself somewhere in the big world, maybe Branson or maybe somewhere even bigger. And I would do my damnedest to give her every possibility of freedom and release from this tiny, backwoods town the two of us had grown up in.

But God must have a bad sense of humor, because all Sicily wanted to do was stay. Stay and find out what in tarnation was going on in Windy Ridge. She wanted to find out why everyone had changed when the fog rolled in, why *I'd* changed.

But the last thing I wanted was for her to stay here, trapped in this town because of me.

Chapter Two

It was about one in the afternoon when I took my break.

And that was saying something because I'd already worked all night. But one of the things about being a vamp was that we rarely get tired. I could go four or five days and nights in a row without feeling the need for any shuteye.

The windows were shuttered closed—you know, because *sunlight*—so I had to watch the clock vigilantly until it was time for me to clock out. Once that time was upon me, I untied my apron, slipped into the back kitchen, and spotted Dorcas Melbourne already sitting at the back table. I tried to keep my face from scrunching too much.

Dorcas, who owned the diner, used to be an old woman. Back then, she was so deaf, we'd had to shout into her eardrums just to be heard. Now, it wasn't much better, because best we could tell, she'd turned into some kind of mole-rat and the rest of her hearing had all but disappeared. That didn't stop *her* from talking, but the rest of us had to resort to improvised sign language and written notes to communicate with her because now she really couldn't hear a darned thing.

Dorcas turned to me as I entered and yelled, "YOU'RE ON LUNCH TOO EARLY."

Her voice sounded like it was coming from the open end of a megaphone. I frowned and shook my head as I took my seat across from her.

"YES, YOU ARE," she yelled back, staring at me from her beady, little eyes. "YOUR LUNCH AIN'T UNTIL ONE."

I sighed, spreading my hands out in front of me. *Yes, Dorcas, I did read the schedule.*

"DON'T SASS ME." Somehow, Dorcas frowned even deeper and pointed to the door with one of her odd, dirt-digging mole claws. The rest of her was covered in satiny grayish-brown fur. "GET BACK ON THE FLOOR OR I'LL HAVE YOU GONE BY THE END OF THE DAY, TWILA." It was a threat she laid on me daily. "I SWEAR, YOU ALL WOULDN'T KNOW A HARD DAY'S WORK IF IT HIT YOU OVER THE HEAD!"

Most days I felt like hitting *her* over the head. With something hard.

I snapped my fingers in front of her eyes, cutting her rant off before my ears started to ring. Grabbing my notepad, I sketched out a quick: *it IS one pm, Dorcas.* and shoved the note in front of her.

She stared at it for a long minute, then huffed, folding her arms and sitting heavily back into her chair.

"YOU DON'T GOT ANY RESPECT FOR THE ELDERLY. I AIN'T NEVER SEEN SOMEONE AS SNIPPY AS YOU, TWILA, WITH YOUR SMART MOUTH RUNNIN' ITS WAY 'ROUND TOWN. NOW, WHEN *I* WAS A WAITRESS BACK IN '57—"

It was easy enough to tune out her rambles, loud as they were. I was much more focused on the ache that had been growing in my head over the last few hours. It wasn't your normal headache; I could feel my veins pulsing inside my skin, twinging like a dehydrated kidney, and that meant one thing: I was getting hungry.

And that was the part I liked least about being a vamp.

In the beginning months, after Sicily returned to Windy Ridge, she studied the newly changed townfolk and determined that I had the fastest speed, hardiest constitution, and most strength out of everyone in town. That *also* meant I had to feed far more often. According to Sicily, the benefits I enjoyed also meant I went through my energy storage quickly, which was more of a hassle than a treasure, in my humble opinion.

If I didn't drink some of the red stuff at least once a day, I turned into a useless heap, but I never let myself get that low—usually because the headaches became too bad to bear. And I didn't wanna risk Sicily being the thing my iron-starved monster mind deemed a good meal. Not that anything like that had happened yet—that was another thing all those vampire movies got mostly wrong—vampires, as far as I was aware, could control our hunger. Yeah, if we didn't eat for a while, we got hangry but no more than any human on a no-carb diet.

But back to my daily need for blood—that was exactly what had gotten me suckered into joining Bud's investigative team. Well, 'investigative team' of sorts. The 'monster hunters' as we'd become known to the folks of Windy Ridge were responsible for weeding out the as-of-yet undiscovered cryptids that wandered the woods.

When the fog rolled into town, it hadn't just affected the townspeople, but it also affected the animals, domesticated or not. So now the forests were full of all sorts of weird creatures that might have started as deer, bears, coyotes or skunks but were now anything but.

Anyway, the monster hunters investigative team was made up of Boone, the now cancerless immortal, Bud, an obese werewolf, and a lizard creature that used to be Ol' Ned. Most of their equipment were traps and snares, but even before the monster business, they set hunting traps in the deeper reaches of the forest pretty frequently.

The team offered me (and the diner) the blood of whatever animals/ creatures they caught if I'd help them with their investigations (having incredible speed, strength and stamina are marketable gifts, apparently) and whatever I couldn't drink right then and there, I bottled and brought to the diner (and wouldn't you know, I was fresh out). There were a few creatures in Windy Ridge who lived solely on blood and none of us were particularly interested in hunting.

Not only that, but human or once-human blood was out of the question where I was concerned. I might have been reduced to this parasitic state, but I'd be damned if I fed on the very people I called my neighbors and friends—especially when they weren't even people any longer. Yes, I could have hunted beyond the hundred-mile-radius of fog-infected towns and woods but I didn't like the idea of taking human blood. Never tried it and never planned to.

I tried not to dread the trip down to Ol' Ned's. To get any kind of food, I knew I was gonna get roped into whatever insanity they'd been cooking up the minute I got there. I didn't *hate* working with them, exactly, but they were a *lot* to deal with on the best of days.

Ol' Ned lived in a trailer just down the lane from mine, both about a ten-minute walk from the diner. In fact, most the people in Windy Ridge lived in the trailer park, though some well-to-dos lived in houses just up the hillside.

The trailer park was called 'River's Edge', and it was the definition of: *sneeze-and-you-miss-it*. Someone could wander through the forest for weeks and never set foot near the place. That was why the monster hunting team had started in the first place; when the fog came, about a quarter of the population lost their marbles and ran off into the woods, never to be seen or heard from again. We'd agreed to try to round up the missing in the hopes of rehabilitating them. And, so far, we'd been able to find about a handful of them and now they were doing good, living their lives as paranormal creatures in Windy Ridge, just like the rest of us.

I'd heard a bit about the team's latest investigation through the gossip of the diner patrons. Apparently, there'd been sightings of a pink man running buck-ass naked through the trees, and Bud and Ol' Ned figured it was a crazy that couldn't hack it. They wanted to trap whatever the thing was, lure it in with a series of baits, then have me wrangle it (superior vampire strength) when they had it subdued.

Because I was the team's strongest member and the hardest one to hurt, they called me in whenever they needed the big guns. And I understood—after all, if anyone else tried to wrangle some of the things I've had to catch, they'd probably be dead before they could blink.

"MY PA USED TO RUN LIQUOR TO BRANSON IN THE THIRTIES, Y'KNOW?"

A sudden word explosion from Dorcas about jolted me right outta my shoes and set my heart to thudding all the way up my throat. Dorcas didn't notice, of course, and I had to sit back and recover as she prattled on.

"RUNS IN THE FAMILY. 'WE GOT BOOZE IN OUR BLOOD' HE USED TO SAY. MY STILL'S GOIN' STRONG, EXCEPT FOR THE DAMN DIP IN SALES. PEOPLE DON'T APPRECIATE GOOD MOONSHINE NO MORE, I TELL YOU WHAT."

I pursed my lips and flipped the notebook, scribbling a note and flipping it towards her. *Most people can't drink anymore, you know that. Monsters don't get drunk like humans do.*

Dorcas looked at the note (how she was able to see anything with such small and sunken eyes was beyond me) and scoffed, the air whistling through her bucked teeth. "THEY JUST AIN'T DRINKING ENOUGH."

I rolled my eyes and shook my head, but before I could reply, I heard something ring in the distance. Instantly, my heart plummeted because that sound could only mean one thing.

"Dorcas! Quiet!" I yelled, forgetting she couldn't hear me.

"WHAT? YOU KNOW I CAN'T HEAR YOU NONE, TWILA! I SWEAR THAT FOG DONE TOOK THE BRAINS RIGHT OUT FROM BETWEEN YOUR EARS!"

I had to wave my hands to make Dorcas stop yelling so I could focus on the sound; deep and low, echoing slightly in the air. It was the town church bell clanging inside its tower, ringing in a steady rhythm of repeated strikes.

There were only a few reasons why the church bell rang. Back when things were normal, it would sound at funerals and weddings. Or occasionally someone would set it off during some important person's christening. Now, though, it was reserved as a warning; *someone had entered Windy Ridge, and that someone was human.*

I stood up, letting my chair tip over behind me.

Grabbing my pencil, I wrote the word "BELL" on a slip of paper and shoved Dorcas out the back of the kitchen. The lunchtime chatter stilled as the other patrons heard the ringing outside, and every single one of them turned to face me as I skidded on the tile, propping the kitchen door open with an old iron bucket.

"We got a normie!"

I ran for a bussing tray, heart pounding as I pointed to the patrons. Nearly everyone inside the diner was some kind of monstrosity. Aside from Sicily and me, the only other person who could pass as normal was Boone.

"You all know the drill!" I yelled. "Anyone who doesn't look human needs to go home, *now!* And don't come back out again until I give you the okay!"

All at once, folk began to stand and rush to the back of the diner as they made for their cars in the lot or just made for home on their feet (the bat-man and gargoyle both flew away).

"Should I help them?" I heard Sicily call at me. I looked over to see her half-standing, eyes wide and books already packed into her bag. Hurrying over to her, I put a hand on her shoulder to sit her back inside the booth.

"No, no, stay here." I peeked through one of the blinds, scanning for unfamiliar faces. Far as I could tell, no one was in the parking lot who shouldn't have been there. It was probably just a matter of time though—if there was a human in town, chances were they were coming here. Everything else was closed. "If everyone's gone, it'll look suspicious. Just... do your work or focus on... on something else, okay?"

Sicily looked unsure but, thankfully, followed my lead with a slow nod. I sprinted around the counter at the unnatural speed I was given, picking up plates of bones and entrails and other distasteful things that outsiders would find puzzling.

Within seconds, the floor was spotless, every trace of unsavory meals dumped out back and shut in the dumpster. All the cryptids were gone and my heart was racing, but I quickly straightened my apron and posed at the counter, tonguing my canines to make sure they were still dormant. As long as they were short, I looked as normal as any human, which meant that in emergencies like this, I was almost always the chosen lookout.

For a long time, Sicily, Boone, and I stayed frozen in our places, the blinds half-open so we could see outside. It was still, silent other than the blood rushing through my ears, but eventually, three figures walked up to the door, pushing it open with a *ching* of the bell tied to it.

They were men, all of them, though their ages varied.

One of them I recognized as Deputy Drayton, a slim man who shifted into a merperson whenever he touched water. Standing next to Drayton was a younger man who was unfamiliar to me—he was maybe in his early twenties. But the last figure made my fingers squeeze into the counter so hard, it nearly cracked.

After all, a girl's likely to get a surprise when her high-school flame walks back into her life after twenty-three years.

Chapter Three

Dean Hawke had grown even more handsome over the years.

He was half Native American, from the Osage tribe, and his olive skin complimented his features, including a strong nose, large and dark eyes, and an elegantly square jawline. His hair was so black as to appear blue in the light and was currently longish, the ends just curling over his collar. It was just as beautiful as I remembered, even with the gray threading up through his temples. Dean had always had a commanding presence, no doubt owing to the fact that he was as broad in the shoulders and chest as he was tall. And, looking at him now, I'd forgotten just how tall he was—easily over six-feet-two. 'Distinguished'… yeah, that was a good word for him.

And the uniform he was currently wearing…

well, that was just icing on an already fit and firm cake. But it was also the uniform that almost surprised me as much as him showing up here... now... as if twenty-three years hadn't gone by or if it had, it had been a mere blink. Even so, I didn't remember him ever showing any interest in becoming an officer of the law, yet that uniform said otherwise. I guess things have a way of changing with time.

The last time I'd seen him was at our senior year graduation. We'd stood, staring at each other as we shared a tearful (and, in hindsight, melodramatic) goodbye. Then Dean had left the county, and while he never said so, I'd assumed it was because the infighting of his family had worsened.

His father had married a white woman, after all, and that hadn't sat well with Dean's grandfather, who had been chief of his tribe. After years of disagreements and anger, Dean had left town. And it was a good thing too because a few months later, a tornado came through our neighboring town of Devil's Run, killing Dean's grandparents, his aunt, and his uncle all at once.

Now, looking at Dean, that tornado, the teary-goodbye, the promises... they all felt like they belonged to another person in another life. I was suddenly overcome by a sadness I couldn't understand. Pushing the feelings back, I swallowed hard as my attention flicked to the younger man standing by Dean's side. As I studied him, I started to realize he did look a little familiar. Mostly because he looked *very* similar to Dean, just with slightly chubbier cheeks and hair that was shaggy and fell into his eyes. At first, I thought the young man had to be Dean's son, but after another bit, I realized it was probably Mason Hawke, Dean's nephew and the only person who'd survived the tornado.

I watched as Dean scanned the diner with those dark and intriguing eyes of his, and when they landed on me, I tried not to flinch.

And it looked like he tried not to flinch.

Just as I expected, his eyes widened, recognition flickering like a flame. It felt like years ticked by in seconds as we just stood there, ensnared in one another's gazes. And then he beamed a grin so wide and so charming, it brought me back all those years—brought me back to a time when he was just a boy and I was just a girl. And we were both standing outside Windy Ridge High School, facing each other—me clutching my textbooks to my chest as I gazed up at Dean Hawke and thought I was the luckiest girl in the whole world to have won this boy's affection. And then Dean would kiss me, like he always did before he had to go to football practice and I'd walk myself home.

I was so dazed, so surprised, so lost in the past, I hardly felt my face flush as we stood there, saying nothing, just staring at each other as the years whizzed by before our eyes.

And then we weren't just standing there. Then Dean was moving, hastily closing the distance between us and I was instinctively taking a step back and then smoothing down the front of my pink uniform, suddenly keenly aware of the hem that had fallen out and the stains on my white apron.

"Twila? I don't *believe* it!" He laughed that deep, loud and joyful sound I remembered so well, and then he was right there—standing right in front of my counter and reaching over to me like he was gonna yank me clear across the Formica tabletop. "Well, come out from behind there! Let me get a good look at you!"

I didn't say anything—it was like I'd swallowed my tongue, but before I knew what I was doing, I was walking around the counter until nothing separated us at all. Nothing but air.

"Dean Hawke," I said, once I could finally find my voice.

He closed the distance that separated us and then his arms were around my shoulders and he was pulling me into the breadth of his chest which seemed, implausibly, to have grown even broader. He held me and I held him and for a second I swear neither of us breathed. But when he pulled me in even tighter and lifted me up, right off my feet, until my face rested in the crook of his neck and I was struck with that scent I knew so well, I felt my head start pounding in earnest. Dean had always smelled like a man of the woods—like musk and forest. And his scent hadn't changed. It had always struck me as the scent of lust, of sex, probably because he was the first man I'd ever had sex with. Now, though, that scent hit me with something else—with a sudden and insistent *want.* No. *Need.*

Hunger. It hit me with hunger.

It had been a very long time since I'd smelled a human other than my own kid. This, though... this was new. I could smell Dean's blood through his skin, and it was like a magnet pulling me towards him, the urge to pull down his collar and go for his throat digging into the back of my head in a way the blood hunger never had before. Immediately, I pushed him away, much harder, in fact, than I meant to.

And he nearly fell over. I could see the shock in his gaze—and I wasn't sure if he was more stunned that I'd abruptly thrust him from me or by the strength with which I'd done it.

"Humm," Deputy Drayton started nervously, reminding me that he and Mason (if that *was* Mason) were still standing there. Sicily and Boone were both staring at me with their mouths hanging open.

Well, damn.

Blushing down to my neck, I forced myself to shove the smell of Dean right out of my head. Furthermore, it was a good thing I'd pushed him away—not only because I needed to control my own blood lust but as a vampire, and contrary to popular opinion, I didn't run cold. I ran hot. Really hot. And I didn't want Dean to notice as much.

Dean, for his own part, seemed to remember himself and cleared his throat like he was embarrassed by his outward display of affection with a woman he hadn't seen in twenty-some-odd-years.

But that sense of wonder was still in his eyes.

And damn those eyes because they were just as expressive as they always had been. Dean may have looked severe at times, but he was one of the most feeling sort of people I'd ever met. When he was angry or happy or sad, you could see the emotion right there in those deep eyes.

"Wow, you—I don't know how it's possible, Twila, but you look exactly the same," he said in a slightly breathless voice. "You're just as beautiful as you were… twenty years ago."

Dean's voice had always been deep, but it was even deeper now.

"I, uh, I could say the… same for you," I answered, irritated with myself because I sounded completely flustered. "Not that you're beautiful," I amended with a very strange laugh.

Dean nodded, but it was like he wasn't really concentrating on the conversation. If I had to guess, he was still stuck in the shock of reuniting after all this time. I was right there with him. Or maybe he was still shocked that I'd just almost knocked him over.

"I didn't expect to see you here… I mean… not in this diner, necessarily, but in Windy Ridge." He cleared his throat again. "After all this time."

I know he didn't intend for me to feel offended, but I did. "Well, some of us never made our way out, I guess you could say." I gave him a little apologetic smile.

"No, I didn't mean," he started, shaking his head and then chuckling lightly at his own blunder as he looked down at the floor. "I'm glad you're here," he said when he looked back up again.

It was my turn to clear my throat. "I, um, I never thought you'd come back."

Dean reached up to smooth back his hair. "Well, I had to come back," he laughed. "I haven't had a good Damnation coffee in years."

"A good Damnation coffee don't exist, Hawke. I swear they water it down," Deputy Drayton said with a faux smile. I noticed the nervousness in his eyes as they flickered to me, a quick flash of apprehension that sent a chill down my spine.

"Now that's a crock o'," I started but lost the words when I noticed from my peripheral, that Boone was standing up and starting our way.

Boone was a tall man, pale in the face as well as the eyes, and always looked a little disconcerting even before the fog had changed everyone. Even though his illness had been taken away from him, he was still hairless from head to toe, which we suspected was a byproduct of the fog's work on him. And even though he still appeared human—a man without hair, eyebrows or eyelashes is a strange sight to behold, let me tell you. Boone still had the tendency to jerk his head to the side whenever he stumbled over his words which was right often. He caught my eye and smiled before he turned to Dean, and I flashed him a grateful smile back—I had a large pocket of fondness for the man, and I knew he likely was coming over to give my monster ass a break.

"Dean Hawke?" He stuck out his hand with a friendly grin. "Why, it-it-it sure is good to see you again." Then he glanced down at Dean's badge and back up again, blinking wide in surprise. "Ossifer."

Dean paused, no doubt surprised by Boone's version of 'officer', but then took the other man's hand with some hesitation before realization suddenly made his eyes brighten. "Boone?"

"That's right."

Dean's grin only widened. "My God, I didn't expect to see you! How the hell have you been?"

"Better than I have b-b-been, Ossifer Hawke." Boone's laugh was high and raspy, either contagious or off-putting depending on where you stood. He spoke in a fast and semi-anxious fashion that made him hard to understand. "Life here's interesting, being in the b-b-backwoods an' all'a that. I got —that is, I was—I caught me a b-b-bad case o' sickness there for a while, and that was a *ride* to g-g-get the hang of."

"A bad case of sickness?" Dean repeated, obviously lost.

"Back five years or so ago," Boone nodded. "The troof of it was, I only h-h-had me a few months to l-l-live."

Dean looked Boone over, and though his expression was impressively hidden with concern, I could tell it was also laced with surprise. "And look at you now, still kicking all these years later!"

Boone clapped Dean on the shoulders with both of his hands. "Prayer is a p-p-powerful thing, Ossifer Hawke." Then he looked over at Deputy Drayton before returning his gaze to Dean. "You a deputy now too?"

Dean chuckled. "Actually, I'm a sheriff."

"Well, con-grat-you-lations," Boone continued, looking as perplexed as I felt.

Dean nodded. "Tell me about what happened with your sickness."

Boone breathed in real deep—whenever he talked about his cancer, he got real serious. "I gotta think someone u-u-up there must—is—er, has been lookin' out for me, Ossifer H-H-Hawke. The chemo reacted real g-g-good an' the last time I saw me the doc, he said I was c-c-cancer free." Boone glanced at me, the slightest twinge in his eyebrow because that was an outright lie. We didn't see doctors here no more because there weren't any doctors to see. "It was a right m-m-miracle, wasn't it, Miss T-T-Twila?"

I nodded. "Oh, yeah. A right miracle."

Dean took a step back and pressed his hands into his pockets, and I watched as he slowly surveyed the diner around him. "Well, I'm glad to hear that, Boone. Speaking of prayer, though, I'm surprised at how empty this place is."

"This place?" I asked, not sure if he was talking about the diner or what.

"Windy Ridge," Dean corrected as he gave me the same smirk he'd given me twenty years ago and the butterflies started up in my stomach just like they always had.

Which was dumb.

"Oh, right," I answered.

"And the diner, too, for that matter," he continued, glancing around himself. "Where are all the churchgoers?"

Dean's question wasn't totally out of left field. There were two churches in Windy Ridge, St. Magdalene was located just down the road from the diner and the other church, All Saints, was on the other side of town. Services used to end at the same time and then all the churchgoers would flock to the diner for lunch. All Saints had to close when the pastor turned into something that resembled a pterodactyl and then flew off for greener pastures. The other pastor, well he was still around, even though he'd turned into a minotaur type creature.

"Ah, well," Deputy Drayton started. "All Saints closed down 'while ago."

"And St. Magdalene doesn't do afternoon services anymore," I said and picked up a rag to clean the counter, trying to seem busy. Talking to Dean was starting to make me antsy, and the hunger in my head was pinging like a pager every few seconds.

"They don't?" he asked, giving me a peculiar expression.

"They don't," I repeated and scrubbed a little harder. "And, well... St. Magdalene is also down for repairs. Don't know when it'll open again, but things *have* been kind of slow in here since."

There was no comment to that so I stopped my

scrubbing and looked up, finding Dean already staring at me. His eyes were piercing, and he wore a soft, unbothered smile on his face that didn't quite reach his eyes. His arms were relaxed, but his stance was steady, and I saw him shift forward ever so slightly, body tense.

A chill ran down my spine because I could tell by his expression that he wasn't buying the load of bullpoop I'd just fed him. Not only that, but the more I talked, the more suspicious he appeared.

I glanced to Boone, and he nodded.

"B-b-by the way, Ossifer Hawke," Boone rested his back against the counter and leaned into Dean's view, "you haven't told us what brings you back to Windy R-R-Ridge."

I looked at Boone and gave him a small nod as a 'thank you' for pulling Dean's attention away from me and my lying butt.

Dean's eyes lit up as he turned to face Boone. "A couple months back, I'd heard Sheriff Grover passed, and the office was looking for someone else to take his place. And, well…" He reached up to his lapel and adjusted a pin there, and in the dim diner light I saw it glint silver in its triangular shield shape. "I guess I took his place." Then he grinned even broader.

I looked at the pin. Boone was staring at me, I could see it from the corner of my eye, but all I could do was look at Deputy Drayton and force myself to breathe. If I didn't focus very hard, I was certain the force of the news would have knocked me right on my behind. What was worse was that the deputy looked just as nervous as I felt.

This was bad. Very bad.

"You took Sheriff Grover's place?" I managed after I figured out how to work my tongue again. Dean nodded, and I could only hope he took my flabbergasted expression as my being happy for him.

"Yeah, after he passed."

Little did Dean know that the sheriff didn't pass... well, not as far as we knew. The fog turned him into what I believed was a troll (Boone thought he was a gnome), but either way, he'd run off into the forest and no one had ever heard from him again. But Dean didn't need to know that.

"Mayor Dooley offered me the job just last week," the sheriff in question continued. "Said the town needed a good fixing up with some law enforcement. He also mentioned that there've been reports of someone harassing some of the neighbors around here, so I decided to stop in to ask folks a few questions." Then he looked around himself. "Only problem is... there aren't any folks to ask."

"Oh, wow... you're... you're back for good." I couldn't keep my voice from shaking. "That's—that's really something, isn't it, Deputy?"

I gave Deputy Drayton my biggest, most pointed stare and then remembered to smile. Every damned member of this town, from the teachers to the gas station employees, had been turned into something supernatural. Even Mayor Dooley himself had a pension for shifting into a squirrel when he got too excited. And he was one of the lucky ones. Most of our townspeople couldn't even shift back into their human forms, so by all waves of logic and sanity, there was *no reason* for the mayor to bring an outsider into our community. Windy Ridge, Devil's Run, and Dagwood had cut themselves off from the rest of the world for the sake of the townspeople's survival. If anyone found out the truth and saw what had happened to the people... well the risks were too awful to even think about.

The deputy smiled and nodded, his voice cheery despite the true terror on his face. "Yes, ma'am. The mayor is full of surprises."

My head throbbed again. Mayor Dooley had lost his *mind*.

I turned to put the rag away, taking the opportunity to gather my wits. There was no use panicking about this now, not when the man I was panicking over was standing right in front of me and waiting for more conversation. I breathed in real deep and told my darn heart to stop beating so loud. I was lucky in that I'd always been told I was hard-to-read, because that meant my tactic of compartmentalizing my issues was working. And so that's exactly what I did—I took my stress, tied it into a little box and dropped it off a cliff, then stood up with an easy grin, shifting my attention to the twenty-year-old at Dean's side.

"Now, if I had to guess, this handsome young

man is Mason Hawke?"

Mason puffed up like a bird, chest out with a look of pride, and I had to choke back a laugh.

"It sure is." Dean put a hand on Mason's shoulder. "Mason here used to work with me back at Branson PD. He's got a gift with a pencil and paper, I'll tell you. Used to be our sketch artist before he decided to come with me to Windy Ridge when I got reassigned."

Boone's face lit up. "You an artist?" Mason nodded. "R-r-really? That's mighty impressive, young man. How l-l-long you been workin' with that art o' yours?"

Mason beamed and shrugged a bit, tossing hair out of his eyes. "Well, I mean—I've been drawing all my life, but I only started working for Uncle Dean when I turned eighteen. Just wanting to help the community where I can, you know?"

I glared at the far-too-interested look on Boone's face and slipped back behind the counter, motioning Dean, Deputy Drayton, and Mason away from Boone. The last thing I needed was those damned hillbilly monster hunters trying to get the sheriff's nephew into their scheme. As nice as it was to see Dean again, it was far, far too dangerous to let either Hawke get close to the truth regarding Windy Ridge.

"Why don't you three sit down and I'll fix you up some coffee and whatever else you've got a hankering for?" I asked, gesturing to a booth in the far right of the diner.

Dean smiled but held up his hand. "While I'd

love to stay and visit, Twila, we'll have to make it three coffees to go. I've got to try to find someone to give me an eye-witness account regarding these sightings I keep hearing about." Then he paused and gave me that crooked smile which made me wish he wouldn't. "You haven't seen anything weird around here, have you?"

Anything weird around here? Ha! That was one way of putting it.

"No, nothing," I lied. Then I breathed in real deep, put my poker face back on and gave him a big, fake smile. "Alrighty. I'll get you three coffees for the road."

"I'd appreciate it," Dean answered and then took a step closer to me. "And I'll definitely plan on coming back to get a proper meal and a proper talk." He paused and there was something hopeful in the dark pools of his eyes. "It's been a long while, Twila Boseman."

"It sure has."

I gave him another quick grin before walking back to the kitchen, letting the door swing shut before I let out the biggest sigh I ever had.

This was going to be *bad*.

Chapter Four

"Summa bitch, Twila, will you stop that pacin' already? You're rockin' the whole trailer. It's makin' me motion sick."

I glared at Bud as I turned around and paced back his way. "That's rich from a man who chases his own tail."

Bud scowled at me from the back of Ol' Ned's double-wide trailer, which was crammed with so much junk, it was hampering my pacing big-time.

Lifting up a can of beer in his paw-like hand, Bud cheersed the air. "Hey, that was one time. What can I say? Moonshine gets me energized."

Normally, Bud's drunken excuses would have had me laughing, but I was way too focused on the dread that had been piling inside me ever since I got here. After Dean, Mason, and the deputy left the Damnation Diner, the adrenaline finally kicked in and I spent the rest of my shift jittering from one end of the place to the other.

Eventually, Sicily convinced me to clock out early since Dorcas wasn't allowed back inside, and we headed over to Ol' Ned's. I wasn't a stress-eater per se, but I sure did inhale the bottles of blood Ol' Ned had waiting for me faster than a drunk with a shot line. The blood took the edge off my senses, but it didn't do too much about the panic.

"You realize how much of a disaster this is, right?" I stopped at the end of the trailer and turned back around to view everyone within. Beside me, Ol' Ned was hunched over his drafting table, his large, lizard-like body barely fitting on the stool. Boone was sitting beside Bud on the couch, which was surrounded by boxes full of any and everything, and Sicily sat on the kitchenette counter, glancing up at me from her cryptid book. None of them were as worried as I thought they should be.

I folded my arms across my chest and glared at each one of them in turn. "This is a massive breach. If Dean finds out what happened to Windy ridge, we're done for."

"We ain't gonna be done for," Bud started.

I shot him a look that took the words right out of his mouth. "We're a town full of *monsters,* for God's sake, if word gets out, we're gonna have the FBI on our behinds before sundown. Need I remind you all that there was a *reason* everyone agreed to let the human-presenting monsters, like me, handle business with the towns outside this one?"

"All I'm sayin' is I don't think Sheriff Dean would go an' do somethin' like that," Bud said.

"And who's to say he won't?" I asked.

"Well, he's Dean Hawke—he grew up here," Ol' Ned said with a shrug.

"Right and he's been gone for over twenty years which means," I started.

"That none of you really knows him anymore," Sicily filled in, giving me a smile.

I shot her back one. "Exactly."

From the back, Boone gave a slow, knowing nod, arms and legs crossed as if trying to slide between the slit in the couch cushions. "An' p-p-people don't like what they don't understand, ri-ri-right, Miss Twila?"

"Exactly," I said as I pinched the bridge of my nose with a bitter sigh. "I just don't get it," I continued as I turned around and paced back down the narrow trail of Ol' Ned's double-wide. "Why would Mayor Dooley put the whole town at risk by hiring an outsider like Dean and threatening this whole town to exposure?"

Bud snorted, tossing back the rest of his beer. "Well, summa bitch, Twila, you knew the mayor was losin' his dang mind. Been on the downward stroke for months."

"I don't think that's all that's going on," Sicily cut in from the side. We all glanced at her and Bud stood up to toss his can into the trash pile which was taking up the entire left corner of Ol' Ned's trailer. Surprisingly, the place didn't smell too bad, probably owing to the fact that Ol' Ned insisted if trash included anything that used to be alive, then it needed to be put in the dumpster at the end of the road. Not that River's Edge had any sort of trash company—we just burned all our trash at the end of every month.

When Bud passed by Sicily, she curled up her nose at him. "Bud, you're a God-fearin' man," she started.

Bud turned to look at her. "Yeah."

"So, do I need to remind you what the bible says about cleanliness?" Then she cleared her throat. "*1 Corinthians 6:20 For you were bought with a price. So glorify God in your body. 1 Corinthians 6:19 Or do you not know that your body is a temple of the Holy Spirit within you, whom you have from God?*"

Bud looked over at me and frowned. "What she goin' on about?"

"I think she's trying to tell you that you stink," I supplied with a shrug.

Bud matched the shrug. "Sorry, Sicily, I'll take me a bath when I get home."

"Thanks, Bud," she answered and gave him a sweet smile.

Boone leaned forward to rest his arm on top of his knee. "What were you s-s-sayin' about the mayor, sugar plum?" he asked Sicily.

She shrugged, pushing up the glasses that had slipped down her nose. "Karen. His wife." I groaned at just the mention of the woman's name. "She's a busybody, as everyone knows."

"Amen to that," Bud put in.

Sicily nodded. "And I'm sure she's got a massive influence over the mayor and that covers a lot of ground. How many times have you heard her goin' on and on about wantin' to be able to leave Windy Ridge and go shoppin' in Branson like a real person?"

"Sure 'nuff," Ol' Ned agreed.

Sicily looked at him and nodded. "Every town meetin' we have, that woman can't keep her trap shut about wantin' to go back to the way things used ta be." She nodded her head and I nodded mine along with her. Then she sighed real hard like. "Even though with that bright red hair and skin, she looks like a used tampon."

"Sicily!" I said, my mouth dropping open.

The boys all snickered in the background as Sicily looked up at me and shrugged. "What? She does!"

"That doesn't mean you have to compare her to a... a... nevermind."

Sicily sniffed and went back to her book.

"She's got a point," Bud said as he scratched at the fur on his jaw. "Shame we can't do much about it though. Far as haughty folk go, Karen's one o' the untouchables."

"Sweet molasses," Ol' Ned started on a sigh as he shook his head. "If she's helpin' that mayor rat us all out, that's some dayum bad news."

I continued pacing, now moving to gnaw on my fingernails with my canines, and Bud stood up and walked to the refrigerator for another beer. He glanced over to Ol' Ned's drafting table to look at the most recent design Ned was working on. "Think you can come up with a snare to catch a catty rich lady?"

Ol' Ned didn't respond. He hadn't looked up from the sketch once except to reach into an open drawer and pop one of the Tums he had stashed there (though, really, I was sure they didn't do much for him). After turning into a lizard man, he'd developed a nasty case of GERD because he refused to switch his diet to insects. Bud poked him again, but he didn't budge, so Bud huffed and placed his palm flat on the drawing, giving Ol' Ned a grin when his head shot up in response.

"Dadgummit, you mutt, yer smudgin' the drawin'!" Ol' Ned slashed at Bud with a reptilian claw but Bud caught it in time, chuckling as he released Ol' Ned and moved his hand again.

"We're havin' us a bit o' a crisis, Ol' Ned," Bud told him. "It'd be nice if you came an' joined us."

"I'm *tryin'* t' figure how to catch this thing," Ol' Ned grumbled back, swishing his tail across the floor. "Whatever's out there stalkin' the trails already got into Miss Green's garden a couple days ago. Nearly had her out while she was plantin' her petunias."

It was by the grace of God that I held in my groan. Ol' Ned had been sweet on Florence Green for years, even before her husband passed and she turned into the wood nymph she now was. So of course, Ol' Ned would be fixated on this case if she was one of the victims. Regardless, we had bigger fish to fry. An' as far as Dean Hawke was concerned, I thought we had us a whole river of bigger fish to fry.

"Look, we don't even know if it's a genuine monster yet," I said and flopped on the couch beside Boone as I gestured outside.

"We know it's been r-r-runnin' 'round outside nekked," Boone said.

I nodded. "That doesn't make it a monster though. It might've just been one of the crazies lookin' for food, or wantin' to see if anything in Florence's garden could get him high. You know how the meth heads have been goin' crazy as soon as they realize their bodies don't react the same way anymore."

Strangely, when the fog came anyone who was on heavy drugs (usually meth out here in the sticks) didn't get physically transformed into anything. They still retained their human bodies but their minds were the things to go. It was like the opposite of what happened to the rest of us—our bodies changed but for the most part, our brains remained our own. For the meth addicts, or the 'crazies' as we called them, they became monsters in their minds, even if they retained their human forms. Regardless, after the fog, their drugs stopped working which probably made their descent into madness even faster.

"Sweet molasses! It wasn't no tweaker," Ol' Ned hissed, frowning. "Miss Green told me the creature had tusks an' bristles an' pink skin. What's more it didn't talk none, wouldn't respond to 'er, and didn't run off 'til she started takin' pot shots at it. He mighta been a crazy, but he's a monster sure enuff. We just don't know what kind yet." Ol' Ned turned and faced Sicily, whose ears had perked up at the sound of a mysterious creature. "I reckon with a few flips o' yer books there, you can find out somethin' about tusk monsters, eh, darlin'?"

Sicily beamed, dog-earing the page in her book. "Oh, for sure. I've got a few new books I got from the library at school, so I'll stay up extra late tonight to see if I can find anything that matches the description."

I choked and stood up, staring at Sicily and Ol' Ned with my brows raised. "You'll do no such thing! It's a school night. You need to be in bed early so you can get up on time."

Sicily's eyes flashed. "What?" she scoffed, and she hopped off the counter with her book in hand. "Come on, Mama, this is important! I wanna help you guys figure out what this thing is!"

"Sicily, your first responsibility is getting your schoolwork done," I said, standing as well. "You can't stay up all night or you'll miss the bus again and then you'll have to walk all the way to Dagwood."

Because the number of high schoolers had dwindled after the fog, Windy Ridge High School had closed and now the only available school was in

Dagwood, which was maybe ten minutes outside of town.

The girl would drive me to drink with the way she kept talking about dropping out of school and getting a GED while turning 'team researcher' into a full-time job, and, of course, I was having none of it. In fact, every time I thought about it, my stomach got all twisty with anxiety.

There had been numerous occasions when I'd had to talk her out of skipping classes to run off with Bud on some new case, and recently, it was starting to cause some tension between the two of us. Call it sappy, but it broke my heart to be at odds with my own kid. A diploma would do her well, and with the brains God gave her, she could land any job. Yet, all she wanted to do was hunt cryptids in the woods of nowhere.

I couldn't help but feel like Windy Ridge was wasting Sicily's brain power and though it would have pained me something terrible, I hoped that someday she'd find her true calling and leave this backwoods town exactly where it belonged—behind her. And if I was lucky enough, maybe she'd take me with her.

"I don't even *need* to be going to school, Mama! Everything I need is in Windy Ridge. Finishing school isn't even *worth* it at this point, an' you know it!"

Something inside me snapped then. It was usually rare that I got what I called my "mama voice" out, but something in Sicily's tone made me march up to her and grab the book right out of her hand.

"Sicily Boseman, I'm not gonna sit here and let you throw away your future before you can even vote. This whole monster-huntin' mess is gonna ruin you one day, and I don't care how much you think otherwise." Then I turned to look at the boys. "She's done for tonight." I turned back to my daughter. "You're goin' home, you're gettin' dinner, and goin' to bed. *Now.*"

There was still adrenaline in my veins, leftover from all the stress and worry I'd suffered earlier, but all of that began to drain when I saw the look of pure fury on Sicily's face. Even so, I pointed to the door, and she turned on her toes towards it, letting it slam behind her and rattle the hinges it hung on.

The trailer went stark silent as Sicily's stomping faded out. I could feel myself deflating, the roaring anger in my head softening to a purr, and I didn't bother to look at the boys around me. I walked to the door, opened it to the cool, fresh air, and taking a step into the night, shut the door behind me as I sat heavily on the porch steps. The evening was calm and quiet, and I could see my trailer just a few rows down, its lights burning a warm yellow across the grass.

Sicily was in there already, no doubt cursing my name all to Hell, and even though I couldn't hear it, I still felt the blows inside my chest. Sicily was so bright that the thought of her wasting her life in a trailer park felt like a crime. But what was an even bigger crime was that she couldn't see what I saw!

How she wanted to stay here was beyond me. I just couldn't understand why. It was hard, upsetting your kid when all you wanted to do was protect them.

Sometimes I thought about sending her to go live with her pa, but I knew that would upset her even more. Alton and I shared custody of Sicily, and all three of us were on good terms until recently, when Sicily decided not to see him anymore. Her decision wasn't out of anything malicious, but more out of worry for him. Sicily had a theory that exposure to the fog could spread outside of Windy Ridge, so she was doing her best to minimize contact with everyone who lived outside town. The last thing she wanted to do was infect her pa, in case that was a possibility. Of course, she couldn't tell him the truth though. Everyone in this town and those neighboring had been sworn to secrecy.

I heard the door open behind me and glanced to the side and saw Boone taking a seat next to me on Ol' Ned's front steps, looking ghostly in the dim light. He smiled, gentle as ever, and reached to put an arm around my shoulder. Boone was a good guy, but I knew he had a thing for me and had for a few years. But he'd never acted on those feelings, and I was grateful for that. I never did feel the same way about him, and every time I looked at him, I still felt bad about it.

I wrapped my fingers around a mug of blood he'd brought out for me. It was cold, which wasn't particularly appealing, but I appreciated the thought and drank a few slow sips as we sat together in silence.

"You alright, Miss T-T-Twila?" Boone asked after a spell. "It's... it's been a r-r-rough few hours for you."

For a moment I thought about lying, but the long day had finally drained me dry, so I shook my head and let it rest in the palm of one of my hands. Then I sighed real long. "... Are you ever scared, Boone?" I asked him softly. The hand on my shoulder tightened a bit and he let out one of his high-pitched, anxious laughs.

"'Course I am. Who wouldn't b-b-be?" I could see him watching me out of the corner of my eye, keeping his gaze gentle. "You musta gotten real s-s-spooked when Ossifer Hawke showed up again, huh?"

I nodded, draining the mug dry. There were a whole lot of thoughts I had regarding Dean Hawke, and most of them I couldn't even identify. Even if I *could* have identified them though, I wasn't going to go sharing them with Boone.

"This is just... so complicated," I sighed. "I don't know how we're gonna keep him from finding us out. There's a million different ways we could expose ourselves now that Dean's in town, and if we do, everything's done for. I thought we were all in agreement that the only human allowed here was gonna be Sicily."

Boone sighed with me and gave a solemn nod. "Somethin' does n-n-need to be done about Mayor

Dooley. But we—but *you*—I'm sure you'll f-f-figure somethin' out, Miss Twila. You always do."

In reply, I gave a wry snort and glanced at him, smirking sarcastically. "You do, do you?"

Boone's eyes shone like moonlight, and he nodded without a shred of doubt on his face. "'Course I do. You—you're as smart as you are b-b-beautiful. An' if anyone can find out a way to keep the new sheriff from messin' everything up, you c-c-can."

God bless him.

I smiled, genuinely this time, and let my head hang. "Thank you, Boone. I appreciate the vote o' confidence. I just… think it's time for this day to be over already."

Truer words had never been spoken.

Chuckling, Boone helped me stand and started walking back towards the front door. "The three of us are g-g-gonna head to the woods t-t-tonight," he said, motioning to the trailer again. "Gonna see if we can f-f-find any scat or tracks the tusk-man l-l-left."

"Have fun on poo patrol," I chided as I raised my hand to say goodbye. "I've got a daughter to pacify."

Boone grinned and waved back, and we parted ways as I walked the short distance back to my trailer and my very angry daughter.

Chapter Five

The next morning, I got up early to walk Sicily to the bus stop.

She usually walked on her own, seeing as mornings and vampire biology didn't mix, but I insisted on joining her to make sure she actually picked up her stuff and went. The nearest stop was miles away, and it was by no means a pleasant experience; the sun made me ache like a bad case of the flu, and with the protective glasses and coat I had to wear, I looked like a wannabe reality star. But it was manageable enough to suffer through, and in addition to making sure she wasn't skipping school, I wanted to keep an eye out in case Dean or Mason Hawke were wandering around nearby.

Sicily still wasn't talking to me by the time I dropped her off at the stop and I did my best not to take her anger to heart. Teenagers would be teenagers. Even though Sicily would be turning nineteen in the spring, it wasn't productive to be fretting over a frustrated child all day. I did get a mumbled "love you" as she hopped onto the yellow bus' steps, and as the bus drove off, piloted by Billy Jenson, a satyr, I toddled my way back to Windy Ridge and tried not to throw up as the sun glared at me from over the mountain ranges.

I entered the town through one of the upper-crust residential areas and spied the Mayor's house from across the road. A three-story Victorian from at least the 1800s, the thing towered over the rest of the houses, which were far more modern, less fancy, and far less expensive.

It was hard for me not to throw the house a petty glare as I crossed in front, on my way home. However, as I did so, something more than ostentatious architecture caught my eye, and I turned to catch a better look. And there was Karen Dooley on her front steps, standing real close to one of her windows and staring at her reflection.

In one hand she held a tube of burgundy lipstick that was a shade or two darker than her body. She seemed to be using her reflection in the window to reapply it. She was dressed in a pretty black number that screamed of flamboyancy. Karen's monstrous transformation had been the most fitting; she'd turned bright red and sprouted horns and a tail, putting on a devilish appearance that matched her devilish insides. And it matched her hellfire temper, as well. She was just a soccer mom before, and she was *still* intimidating as all get out. Now, she had the looks to go along with the temperament.

Karen didn't have a human form to shift back into, so like most of the people in town, she usually stayed indoors, which was why seeing her pressed up against her outside window made alarm bells start ringing in my head. I paused, hesitated, then crossed back over to her lawn. She didn't notice me, which I expected, considering how engrossed she was with herself, so I took the opportunity to stand in the shade of her house, directly behind her.

"Karen."

She jumped so hard, I saw her nick her tooth on the tip of the lipstick. The laugh I held back died as soon as she turned around and put her blackened eyes on me, pinpricks of red serving as pupils in pools of oil.

"Twila! God above, what is wrong with you? Don't you know better than to go sneakin' up on folk like that?" she drawled, bringing a hand to her chest. She put the top back on her lipstick and unceremoniously scrubbed the mark from one of her fangs with a finger.

"I don't have the time to tell you all the things that are wrong with me," I started, eyeing her real narrow like.

"Is there a *reason* you're invading my lawn this morning? I thought you were nocturnal."

"I am," I replied grumpily, tugging the coat tighter around me. "I was walking my daughter to school. The better question is: why the hell are you outside? Last I checked, it wasn't Halloween."

Karen raised a dainty brow and placed her makeup back into her bag. "Why shouldn't I be?"

"Because your husband hired a *human* to be our new sheriff." I couldn't stop the anger from creeping into my voice as I gestured to one of the manor windows. "And, considering the conversation I had with our new sheriff yesterday, he's got no clue about the fog and what happened to us after it came through. If he sees you, that's gonna start a whole mess of issues if you don't give him a heart attack first."

To my surprise, Karen *snorted*, and then rolled her eyes in reply, a snarky smile taking up her mouth.

"Oh, honey, I *know* Sheriff Dean is here," she said, smiling at me like I was the one not in the know. "It wasn't *my husband* that went through the trouble of getting him to come to town, you know."

For a while, I just stared at her, mouth open like a gasping fish. My hands twitched, and I had to restrain myself from letting them clamp down on her throat. Steeling myself with a deep breath, I had to take another one before I could form words again. One thing I could say since becoming a vamp, my temper was a heck of a lot hotter than it had been.

"What," I said slowly, closing the distance between us, "are you talking about, Karen?"

Karen faced me and shifted her weight so her hip stuck out. Then she proceeded to look at me like I was the dumbest person she'd ever met. "I'm surprised you assumed *my husband* was the one who brought the sheriff to town."

"And why *wouldn't* I think that?" I took a step closer.

She just glared at me. "Because he can't do anythin' without *my* help. I've been talkin' to him about gettin' a new sheriff for months, an' did you see a new sheriff anywhere?"

"No, I sure didn't."

She nodded. "So, I went through the trouble, for the sake of *our town*, and got us a new one to take care o' everythin' that's been so outta hand."

"What's happened that you could deem 'out of hand,' Karen?" I demanded, wrapping my arms against my chest because I was just an itty-bitty inch away from wringing her darned neck. "The investigative team has been takin' care of any threats to us for the past *year.*"

"Hmph."

I folded my arms even tighter. "Windy Ridge is now almost entirely self-sufficient. And might I remind you, there's a *reason* we haven't gotten a new sheriff yet, *Karen*." I pointed at her. "And you're one o' those reasons!"

Karen's mouth worked itself into a knot. She flipped her dark red hair over her shoulder, trying to appear nonchalant even though I could see her shifting from foot to foot. I wasn't sure, but I had me a good idea that devils didn't have very good tempers. Probably on par with vampires.

"Well, sure, that might be so about Bud's team,"

she started, narrowing her coal-black eyes at me. "But there *may* have been another reason for me doin' what I did."

"And what reason would that be?"

She jutted her chin out. "We're all sick of being cooped up in this tiny little town, all cut off from the outside world. Not a single one of us can go more than a hundred miles outta this miserable place, and I just can't *take* it anymore, Twila! It isn't healthy, none of this is, and I've had enough!" She slammed her chin up in the air so I could see right up her nostrils. "An' I'm takin' a stand!"

None of this was news. Just as Sicily had said, Karen had been going on and on like this ever since the beginning of the post-fog era. She was one of the folks that nearly bolted into the woods, unable to accept her change. Mayor Dooley managed to talk her down, but none of us really thought she ever quite got over what had happened to her.

I actually thought she was a nutjob, because she alternated between believing that none of what had happened was actually real (there were days when she'd insist she was the same as she'd always been) and other days when she'd start accusing the rest of the world of not accepting her for the way she was. I was fairly sure her mind was slipping, and she veered in and out of reality. Sometimes, when I thought about it, I did feel bad for her, because it wasn't as though she could get help for her kind of crazy. Mental health professionals weren't a thing in Windy Ridge, and it wasn't like she could just waltz into a therapist's office, looking like… well, like a used tampon.

However, I also knew Karen was spoiled, and she missed going on her expensive vacations and spending taxpayer money on salon trips. Which made the anger that rose in me feel *far* more understandable. Yep, my temper was starting to get the best of me. And the heat rising in my cheeks had nothing to do with the sun.

Before I could fully register what I was doing, I advanced on her, blood rocketing to my ears. "Do you have *any* idea what you've done here?" I demanded as she staggered back against her front door in surprise.

Bud had told me on more than one occasion that I was the scariest when I was quiet. Now, my voice hissed out from behind my teeth and I could see Karen's pointed ears flatten like a dog's at the rasping sound.

"You've just put every single person in this town in an *insane* amount o' danger," I continued. "I always knew you were selfish, but this—well, I never thought you'd do somethin' as terrible as this, Karen Dooley."

Karen bristled, though she still cowered beneath my shadow. "I haven't done anythin' that's goin' to hurt anyone! Instead, I brought in a sheriff to protect us all!"

"Against what, Karen?" I almost yelled at her. "We're the monsters!"

"Speak for yourself." Karen tried to straighten,

meeting my eyes with her squinting, beady black ones. "You'll never understand, Twila, because *you* never got outta this awful town. So, you don't know there's a wonderful, wide-open world out there."

"I know plenty about there bein' a world outside o' this one."

"Well, it isn't natural for us to stay cooped up in this town with nowhere to go! It's not fair! It's high time for the world to realize that things like shifters an' vampires exist."

"Listen to what you're sayin', Karen."

She started shaking her head, and that crazed look in her eyes only grew. "I know they'd accept us if they learned the truth an' if they realized we are all still God-fearin' sorts! If they could see we might look different but we're still the same on the inside! All we have to do is jumpstart the process an' show the rest o' the world that we aren't a threat, that we're all still human underneath it all."

My entire body felt like it was in flames, my jaw clenched with painful fury. "Karen, you—"

"I'm done entertainin' your simple mind, Twila." She then stuck her nose up at me and stepped to the side, swishing my legs with her pointed tail. "I have a lunch date with Sheriff Dean in fifteen minutes to set him straight about everything that's happened here, an' there isn't anything you can do about it."

Then my mouth really did drop wide open as I imagined Karen walking into the diner and Sheriff Dean seeing her. And there was no way that was going to happen. Not on my watch.

She tried to walk past me, but my hand shot out before I could think about it. My fingers wrapped around her arm as her knees started buckling under my iron grip.

"I beg to differ."

Karen screamed. Then she tried to pull away, but my strength against hers was no contest. I turned and pushed her back against the door, using my jacket sleeve to muffle her as I scrambled for the doorknob. Opening the door, both of us fell into the Dooley's living room, Karen on her back and me right on top of her.

It was January, but the living room was still decked out in gaudy Christmas decorations, and I had to kick over a statue of St. Nick before I could slam the door shut with my foot. Then I tried to grab onto Karen's shoulder to yank her up again, but she shifted and I ended up grabbing a fistful of her hair. As soon as I let go of her mouth, she launched herself upward and thrust the tip of her ram's horn into my mouth.

Splitting pain careened down my jaw and destabilized me just enough for her to push me to the side. I tasted blood and looked up as Karen scraped her hooves against the hardwood and scrambled up. I jolted forward and managed to catch her around one ankle, but she grabbed onto a Nutcracker from a side table and slammed me over the head with it. The splinter of wood echoed inside my ears, but thankfully I was much heartier than a cheap Christmas decoration, so I was still able to pull her to the ground and find a handhold in the curve of her horn.

She yelled again as I pressed her face into the floorboards, her claw-nails digging into the fabric of my jacket.

"Dustin!"

I glanced to the side, to the table that had the nutcracker on it, and grabbed the runner on top. "Oh, no, you don't."

Ripping off a sizable swath of fabric, I then wadded it up, so it was the size and shape of my fist and then forced her jaw open so I could shove it in, careful not to smother her in the process. Then I didn't hesitate in taking her wrists in my hands and dragging her over to the Christmas tree in the center of the living room. On it, lights twinkled in a dainty juxtaposition to the brawl we were having, and I looked down at Karen's writhing form as I wrenched the lights off the fir branches.

"I'm not going to—" I panted while wrapping the wires around her wrists, blood trailing from my injured mouth and all over Karen. "Let your stupidity an' selfishness—" I ran the line down to her ankles, pulling them in tight, "risk the lives of everyone in this town!"

I pulled the wires taut and stepped back. Karen was now on her stomach in a perfect hog-tie, whimpering through the makeshift gag, and her eyes kept darting over to the door in what I initially thought was a futile plea to escape. I knelt down just to make sure she could still breathe, but as I did so, I managed to catch something as it flashed across my periphery. My head jolted up in time to catch a fluffy brown tail scurrying underneath the couch, and just briefly, a pair of black rodent eyes turned to me, a gray streak of fur making a mustache on its top lip.

Mayor Dooley.

I dove for the door just as the squirrel rocketed toward it, though I knew the mayor wouldn't be able to open the door without shifting back to his human form. He was slippery, far more dexterous in his squirrel form, but I still managed to grab hold of his bushy tail before long and lifted him up into the air. He reared back and sunk his teeth right into my hand.

"Ouch!" I screamed as I released him from my hand and then carried him like a mama cat carries her babies so he wouldn't bite me again. Then I walked the mayor into their dining area. There was an old hamster cage still stuck in the corner, from a time when Mayor Dooley used to have pets (before he became one). I tossed him inside and closed the lid tightly. Then I took a deep breath and glanced down at my hand, noticing how the puncture wounds were already knitting themselves closed. Sometimes it was good to be a vamp.

"You and your wife are a hazard to this town," I said as I looked down at the mayor in his cage. "Maybe after you have some time to calm down, you'll remember who's keeping both o' you from bein' strapped to a laboratory table in some government office."

The mayor shot me a fierce little squirrel look before jumping on his hamster wheel and running like he was trying to break free of his cage using the wheel.

I turned to face his wife as she shot me a fearful look when I passed her by. I won't lie in saying that a surge of triumph coursed through me, barely muting the anxiety as I shut the door behind me.

Chapter Six

I took a somewhat faster route home as I left the Dooley manor.

Panic had settled inside my gut like an anvil and I rushed to my trailer, tossing my coat and glasses on the back of the chair. My head was pounding something fierce, owing to the fight Karen had put up. And there was blood all over the front of me.

Wonderful. Just wonderful.

I was well aware of the trouble I'd be in if Mayor Dooley or Karen managed to escape from their bindings, but to be fair, I still didn't think I'd had much choice in the matter. It was either a few days in county jail with Deputy Drayton on watch or a lifetime in the clutches of the government. And I'd seen enough of the X-Files to definitely opt for the jailtime.

Soon, I was out the door again, dressed in my

Damnation Diner uniform—a pink dress with white apron and short, bloused sleeves and a hemline that reached right above my knees. Not the sexiest getup ever, but who said a waitress was supposed to look sexy? Better question—why was I even thinking about whether or not my uniform was 'sexy' when the subject had never occurred to me before? I was more than sure the answer had something to do with a certain tall, broad and dark-haired gentleman who'd just walked back into my life.

Speaking of my vanity, I took a quick look in the mirror just to reassure myself that the wounds I'd suffered with Karen were healing. They were, but not as quickly as I might have liked. Another few hours, though, and they'd be as good as gone. As to why I decided to give myself a splash of blush, a touch of mascara and some lip gloss? I wasn't sure. Actually, I was, but I didn't want to think about it.

As I walked to the diner, I searched for any shade I could find and tried to nurse my headache with promises of downing a glass of blood once I got to work. Ol' Ned had promised he'd drop off a few bottles this morning. Hopefully he'd held true to that promise because I was in desperate need of something to take care of the steady droning between my ears. I was lucky the diner wasn't too far away from River's Edge. Without my protective gear, I wouldn't have been surprised if the sun cooked me into a pork chop within the hour.

Yes, I had a car, but it wasn't running currently.

As I finally reached the diner's parking lot and

pushed my way through the double doors, I spotted the sharp features of Dean Hawke where he was sitting in one of the back booths, accompanied by Deputy Drayton once again.

When I walked in, Dean glanced up from his coffee, smiled, and I got the distinct impression, he'd been sitting there, waiting for me. I had to fight down a blush as I threw a smile back at him and reminded myself it was definitely NOT a good thing that my old flame was back in town. In fact, it was a very bad thing.

Only one other person was scheduled to work today and I caught sight of her as soon as I slipped through the kitchen door. The smell of bacon grease and biscuits wafted up from the stove where a girl was stationed, plump and freckled but surprisingly muscular.

Hannah was her name, and she was a were-fox. She was also a student who was struggling to keep up with her online high school degree ever since she'd turned shifter (she had anxiety and didn't do well with mixing with other cryptid students so Dagwood High was out and an online degree was in). Now, she turned to face me and smiled, wearing one of my specially designed hats to keep her furry ears hidden and a specialty pair of pants to keep her tail hidden.

"I was wondering when you were gonna get here," she said, and cocked a ginger brow at me. "Jeez, that's a nasty mark you got there."

I froze. "Shoot, did I have a bruise?"

Not waiting for her to answer, I rushed to the restroom and glanced at the mirror over the sink. Sure enough, I spotted a dull purple oval where Karen's horn had ripped into my mouth. "Shoot, shoot, *shoot*," I said as my heart started beating double-time and I hoped upon hope that Dean hadn't noticed the bruise when I'd walked in. And dang it all but the mark hadn't been there when I'd left home —but that was part of healing extra fast—the bruising also came on extra fast.

"Uh—Hannah, d'you have extra concealer I can borrow for a second?" I asked as I walked back into the kitchen and beelined straight for the small refrigerator in the back, where the diner kept the stock of blood. Just as Ol' Ned had promised, there were a few glass bottles waiting for me. I grabbed one, popped off the top and downed it in four seconds. The blood would also help to heal me a little faster.

Hannah passed by me and reached into her purse, but her expression had grown concerned as she walked over to hand it to me. "What's going on, Twila? Are you alright?"

"I'm not *amazing*, I'll be honest." She handed me a little compact mirror and looking into it, I slathered the makeup over the bruise on my lip, wincing, and turned to her. "Look, we've got a situation."

"A situation?"

I nodded. "Apparently, Karen Dooley was the one who wanted Sheriff Dean to transfer here."

"That woman is going to be the death of us,"

Hannah answered, sighing as she shook her head.

I nodded mine. "Not if I have anything to say about it."

Hannah eyed me real narrow like. "What did you do, Twila?"

"I just had an... *altercation* with Karen after she told me she was planning on meeting Sheriff Dean, *in person*, so the rest of the world could find out the truth about us."

Hannah's face went pale, and I thought I saw her ears fold down underneath her cap. "Seriously?"

"Seriously." I prayed the concealer would be enough to avoid any questions Dean might have about what in the heck had happened to me. And that reminded me...

"Listen, Hannah," I started. "I need you to do me a big favor."

"Okay." She had the good sense to look concerned about what that big favor might be.

I sighed, long and hard. "When I said '*altercation*', I mean I left both Karen and the mayor trussed up in their house. I can take over things here to make sure the sheriff doesn't find out anything, but I need you to go and make sure Karen and the mayor stay put." I was fairly sure neither one of them was going to break free anytime soon, but I wanted to be extra careful. This was one of those situations I couldn't afford to screw up. "Think you can handle that?"

Hannah's auburn eyes narrowed in thought. I

felt a little bad for asking her to babysit the Dooleys for me, but then remembered the time we'd caught a crazed dryad inside Hannah's parent's trailer and Hannah managed to knock the dryad out and then tied her up with her own vines. The girl could handle herself and then some, which was why I stopped feeling so bad and started feeling relieved when she grinned and stuck out her hand like we were gonna shake on it.

"Only if you'll knit me another hat," she said. "This one doesn't match everything."

"Deal." I took her hand and shook it. "Lock their front door when you get there an' make sure Karen knows if she tries anything, she's gonna answer to me." Hannah nodded and hurried out the door, and I waited until she was out of sight before taking a long, steadying breath and making my way back onto the diner floor.

"Howdy, boys." I raised my notepad in greeting as I approached Sheriff Dean and the deputy. They both looked up and, again, Dean hit me with that smile of his that made me feel like my knees were made of rubber.

"Twila! Good to see you this morning." Dean looked me over then, brows bent in confusion. "I'm surprised you're here."

I laughed. "Well, I do work here."

He laughed. "No, I meant... Why are you on shift this morning? You were working here last night."

That made me smile. Partially from his concern, but mostly from the fact that he'd obviously never worked in food service before. "Oh, sometimes you gotta work doubles if you wanna make the big bucks," I laughed, feeling uneasy under his gaze. In fact, my neck was starting to heat underneath my collar and I had to think back over whether or not I'd remembered my deodorant this morning. Yes, vampires got just as sweaty as the next person. "This place needs the help, anyway."

"What happened to the other girl who was here a second ago?"

"Hannah's still in high school so her schedule is a bit... wonky," I answered with a shrug, wishing Dean didn't ask so many damned questions. But he'd always been like this—right inquisitive. "She needs the flexibility, and I don't mind. Like I said, I need the hours, since I've got Sicily to take care of and everything."

"Sicily?"

And that was when I realized he had no clue that I had a daughter. "Oh, I... I have a daughter."

"Do you?" His eyes seemed to go even wider and his smile grew.

"I do."

"And her name's Sicily?"

"It is."

"Interesting name."

I nodded.

I'd always wanted to visit Italy ever since I was a little girl. But life isn't like the movies and the truth of the matter was that I'd never made it out of the Ozarks. So, I had to settle for naming my only daughter after Italy, rather than ever traveling there. I'd made my peace with it.

"Very pretty name," Dean continued, scratching at his stubble which was suddenly the sexiest thing I'd ever seen on a man. Even though it seemed like he wanted to say more, he lost the thought and, in response, I raised a brow at him. He cleared his throat. "You said you needed the extra hours..."

"Right."

"Does... does *your husband* not... help you out?"

The fact that he was clearly hanging on my response made me nearly want to laugh out loud, until I reminded myself that Dean being back in Windy Ridge was bad, not good.

It's bad, Twila, not good.

"Actually, I'm not married."

"Ah," he nodded and I swear that smile broadened. "Imagine that."

I wasn't sure what that meant, but just smiled at him and wished I wasn't blushing so darn hard, but I could feel the truth in the heat of my cheeks. "Alton, that's Sicily's dad, well..." I cleared my throat. "Well, we broke up a good few years ago. We're still friendly, and I still like to see him every now and then, but we were never serious enough to get married."

Just serious enough to have a kid together.

Yes, I was well aware how silly my comment sounded but it was already out my mouth and there was nothing to be done for it now.

"That's good. I'm—well, I'm glad you two are still on good terms."

There was something in his voice that made the inside of my collar heat up even more. Something in how his eyes locked on mine, crinkling happily at the edges. Well, I wasn't sure, but I thought he almost looked... relieved.

That was a thought I quickly shook from my head. No time for fanciful thinking, especially with a very human Sheriff Dean. Besides, even if he *was* interested, nothing could happen between us. It was too dangerous, for me and the rest of the town. And it was too dangerous for him, seeing how he was still human. Yes, what needed to happen right away was that Sheriff Dean needed to return to wherever it was he'd come from. I just wasn't exactly sure how to make that happen.

"So," I cleared my throat and tapped my pad with my pencil. "Some scrambled eggs and coffee to go? Maybe some bacon?"

Deputy Drayton leaned toward me. "I'll have my, uh, usual," he said, giving me a meaningful look. Being a merperson meant the deputy lived on a diet of algae and fish, but seeing as he was probably spending a lot more time around humans lately, he had to feed a little more discretely.

"One breakfast burrito, got it." I tossed him a wink and turned to Dean. "And you, Sheriff?"

"The eggs sound nice. And I won't turn down a refill on my coffee." He grinned, leaning back on his booth seat.

"To go?" I continued and didn't mean to sound so hopeful but having Dean around me—well, it did a number on my nerves and my nerves were already frayed enough as it was.

"Oh, I'd like to have both here, if you don't mind."

I scribbled down the orders and did my best to look surprised. "I thought you two were busy with eyewitness accounts and all that?"

"We are. We're meeting one in a few minutes, actually." As he said the words, Dean leaned to look out the window and scan the sidewalk. "If you could help keep an eye out for Karen Dooley, I'd appreciate it." It was at that point that Deputy Drayton gave me an expression that said he was panicked at the prospect of red, horned Karen walking through the door, but didn't know what to do about it.

"Karen Dooley," I repeated, nodding.

"I can't get any cell service out here," Dean continued as he checked his phone again and then shook his head. "And the last time I was able to contact Karen was from the station landline." He turned back to me with a humored smile. "It's been ages since I actually had to look someone up in the phone book. I had to grab the one in the station we were using as a doorstop."

There was a brief pause, and I realized he'd expected me to laugh. I was so caught up in my nerves though that I was hardly paying attention, so the stifled, choked noise I made in response probably wasn't as convincing as I hoped.

"You know, I actually live right by the Dooleys," I said, flashing Deputy Drayton a look that said I had everything under control even though I wasn't sure I did. "I heard Karen and her husband came down with a nasty stomach bug last night." I gave a non-committal shrug. "I'll keep an eye out for her, but I don't think she'll be coming in here anytime soon—not if she was as sick as I heard she was. These things can take a few days to pass, you know."

I watched Dean's expression shift, slightly, and a bit of anxiety tugged at my gut. "Really," he said, a flat statement rather than a question. "Well. That's a shame."

"You, uh, you want me to leave her a message? I can drop it off on my way home?" I offered, hoping he'd take me up on it and that would be the last of that.

"No, no, I don't want to bother you, Twila," he answered and nodded, that piercing gaze of his never leaving mine. When Dean looked at you, he didn't just see you—he studied you, everything about you—the way you breathed, the words you said, the inflections you said them with, the way your eyes creased or didn't crease. He was always taking everything in and, at the moment, I could see he was doing exactly that to me.

"It's no bother," I started.

"I can head up to the station again and leave her

a voicemail," he almost interrupted. "She seemed really... concerned about something. Something she said was important, so I want to follow up."

He was staring at me like he could see directly into my head. All of a sudden, I felt like no matter what I said next, he wasn't going to believe it, something which made zero sense because he didn't even know me—not anymore. A person can change a lot in twenty years.

Except you're just as bad a liar as you always were, I argued with myself.

Speaking of, I knew I had to fib about Karen. I hated telling a mistruth, but as one of the few human-looking monsters in a hundred miles, lying was something I'd had to get used to. But lying to Dean... well, it just felt extra dirty. Strangely.

"Fellas, do you mind if I have a seat?" I put my notepad in my apron and gestured to the cushion across from Dean. Dean looked surprised, but Deputy Drayton scooted over at once, and I slowly joined them at the table.

"Everything okay?" Dean asked, and I sighed, placing my hands on the table in front of me as I told myself not to break my poker face. And not to look into Dean's eyes because the second I did, I was more than sure he was gonna read the truth right in them.

"I didn't wanna say this because I don't want to spread gossip," I started and focused on Deputy Drayton, who was looking at me like he half-expected me to turn into a bat and fly away. "But if Karen's gone to the sheriff now..." I looked over at

Dean, real quick. "To you..." I looked back at Drayton. "Well, then, I feel like this needs to be said." I leaned closer as if worried the other patrons might overhear me, just to sell the lie a little more. "It's kind of known that Karen's a bit... well, she's got some *issues* she's trying to work through."

"Issues?" Dean repeated, his eyes narrowing on me.

"Right." I nodded. "Karen isn't what I would consider... mentally stable."

"She's not?"

I nodded again and then realized I should have been shaking my head. So I did just that. "She's been having bad luck with doctors for a while and things have started to get a little... worse."

At this, Deputy Drayton seemed to pick up the story I was spilling and nodded real enthusiastic like, arching his fingers on the table. He then cast a concerned look at the sheriff as he continued nodding, this time with gusto.

"We've had a few false reports from Karen in the past," he said.

Dean looked at him. "You didn't mention that."

The deputy nodded. "I didn't bring the, uh, reports up because I, uh, well... I want to take everyone's accounts as the gospel truth."

"Even when they aren't," I nearly interrupted. "Karen's been known to... *see* things."

"See things?" Dean repeated, narrowing his eyes like he wasn't following me.

"I'm afraid that whatever she might have called you about was nothing more than her own paranoia," I continued, giving him a sigh. "I don't mean to discount her totally, but... Karen's a little... off her rocker, if you know what I mean."

Honestly, I'd expected Dean to take the lie without a thought. It was perfectly reasonable, and technically, nothing I'd said was explicitly *false* because Karen was so far off her rocker, she wasn't even still standing on the porch. But when I looked back at his face, his expression had darkened significantly. Darkened into something angry.

Dean leaned in towards me, and I felt those eyes once again piercing right into my soul.

"Twila," he started softly, "Why are you lying to me?"

Everything went cold.

I didn't look at the deputy but I saw him pale out of the corner of my eye as I straightened up, hoping to swallow down the choked feeling in my throat. "What d'you mean?"

"I'm no idiot." Dean straightened, mirroring me, with his hands flat on the table. "And I know you aren't one, either."

"I never meant to imply," I started but he interrupted me as he shook his head, spearing his cross expression between me and the deputy. "This isn't the same town I left all those years ago. Is it normal for things to change? Sure. But what's *not* normal is for an entire population to be cut in half in the span of twenty-three years."

"Cut in half?" I repeated as my heart did its best

rendition of a jailbreak—my ribs being the jail cell.

Dean, meanwhile, gestured to the window, where the empty noonday streets stared back at us, almost accusingly. "This place is a ghost town. No one is out on the streets, and anyone I *do* come across seems to want to stay clear of me. People around here are acting strange—like it's them against the world, and that isn't the Windy Ridge I remember."

"Hmm," I started, not really sure what more to say, because it wasn't as though I could agree with him.

"People outside Damnation County have been reporting infrequent contact with their loved ones for the past year," Dean continued, that annoyed expression of his still in full force. "If they weren't cut off from their loved ones entirely, that is. And there are rumors of numerous missing people from this town. It's like one day half the population just disappeared and no one can explain why… or even seems to want to try."

I was still as Dean paused to take a breath. When he looked at me again, I felt my skin start crawling like a mouse's when staring down a hungry cougar.

"This can't be a coincidence," Dean continued. "And the fact that you're making excuses means you know something I don't—something *you don't want me to know*."

I glanced at Deputy Drayton. He was shaking in

his seat, eyes glued to the side of the sheriff's head. Dean pressed forward again, and in my shock, I didn't realize he was going for my hand until his fingers grazed it. By instinct, I wrenched my hand away and clutched it to my chest. But Dean had already touched me and that meant he'd already felt the temperature of my skin and, just like I'd feared, his eyes were round with surprise.

Another thing that contradicts typical vampire lore is body temperature. Most people assume I'm cold as ice, maybe even a little stiff from post rigormortis, but that isn't the case for any of the monsters in Windy Ridge. I can't feel it, but according to Sicily, I run at around 105° Fahrenheit, burning hot most days. Sicily figures it's just another sign of my increased metabolism, but no one really knows for sure.

When Dean touched my hand, I knew he'd felt the heat radiating off me. And this time, I didn't have a flustered hug to explain it away.

I stood. "Excuse me, guys, but I gotta get back to work. Those tables won't bus themselves." My head was down, and as much as I wanted to help Deputy Drayton come up with an excuse as to why I was acting so weird, I had no idea where to begin.

Everything inside me was screaming, panic clawing from within my throat. I turned and rushed back towards the kitchen. There was no way I could make this look *less* suspicious, not on my own, and not with the mess that was facing me now. Of course, Dean would have noticed the changes to the town! He was a sheriff, for crying out loud! He was trained to do exactly that—to notice when things didn't add up.

As I shoved into the kitchen, my hands gripping my apron so tight, my nails pierced the fabric, I collapsed against the nearest countertop. This was the first time I'd started to hyperventilate since I'd learned I had fangs, and as I tried to control my breathing, my brain kept shifting to one thing and one thing only.

If Karen Dooley managed to get us locked up in some government bunker, I'd rip off her horns with my own bare hands.

And that was when I heard something.

I stopped the train wreck that was my thoughts and, instead, listened real good, trying to hear if someone had followed me. But when I glanced back, I realized no one had. And what I'd just heard hadn't come from the outside door.

I froze, as beside me, I heard the clanging of pots and pans, noises my panic hadn't allowed me to register before. Something snuffled, then squealed, then there was the sound of feet or paws or hooves thudding against the floor.

Rushing me.

Now, I'm not generally a screamer.

But when I saw that huge, pinkish blob rocketing towards me, my breath returned in a long, high, frightened shriek.

Chapter Seven

"Get out as fast as you can," I said to Hal, the cook and his two helpers who were already on their way out.

As soon as they disappeared, I could only watch as the thing charged me.

In my rush to get to the diner, I'd made the bad decision to wear low-rise heels—they were good for tips, but *very* bad for floor traction. So, I wasn't surprised when a patch of something on the slippery floor caught my heel and I lost my balance, falling right as the thing aimed a headbutt at me, but luckily, smacked into the charbroiler of the grill station instead.

Whatever it was, it was huge, angry, and moving *way* too fast.

I was dazed, shocked and panicked, but survival mode had kicked in enough for my thoughts to be clear; *if that thing had hit me, it would have knocked me out cold, no question.* I was strong, sure, but a blow to the head can take anything or anyone out if the creature delivering the blow was strong enough. And I was fairly sure this one was beyond strong enough. Just a few months ago, I'd been knocked out cold for an hour or so while we were chasing down Pastor Greg, the holy man-turned-minotaur. Boone had to shoot the pastor with a buckshot to keep him from goring me.

This thing, however, was *not* a minotaur.

I managed to catch a better look at its face as it stumbled back from the impact with the charbroiler, and weirdly, the thing looked more human than monster. It had arms and legs, no hooves or claws. Its face, though, was less human with bristles poking out from its bright pink skin, and two curling tusks jutting out from either side of its mouth. It most resembled a hog. It may have had more unusual features, but most of its face was smeared with whatever it had been feeding on in our kitchen —bacon grease and raw eggs dripping from its jowls. It was easy to figure out why the creature had found its way back here; the back door to the kitchen was broken and thus, hung on its frame which meant for an easy break-in. That, and there was no better place to get a ton of food than a diner.

I rolled away, kicking my shoes off as I tried to stand again, but the hog-man saw my movements and charged me again. With hardly enough breath left in my lungs to scream, I did manage to dodge the thing and this time, it went skittering to the other end of the kitchen, crashing into the freezer, where it lost its footing and slammed into the linoleum floor. While it was down on the ground, I caught sight of its bleeding knees and the scarred skin on the bottom of its hands. Even in the midst of the chaos, both of those injuries stood out to me because they hinted to the fact that this thing hadn't retained its human mind. Most of the 'civilized' monsters or shifters of Windy Ridge were sentient enough to put on clothing or some form of protection to keep their skin from getting torn up.

Of course, I couldn't think about much for long, because the thing was back on its feet again and launching itself at me and I was scrambling just to stay out of its way. Part of me was disappointed in myself because I'd faced far worse than naked hogmen in the past, and I had no doubt that if I could just get a second or so's thinking time in, I could take him down no problem. In the past, though, I'd always had the backup of Boone and the boys.

I managed to climb to my feet after ducking away from another headbutt and vaulted around the fry station, tripping over a fry basket that had landed on the floor. Losing my footing, I crashed into the ground, tweaking my foot and busting one knee wide open. The stab of pain that shot up my leg caused me to cry out, but instead of getting rammed by a pair of tusks, I felt a pair of hands underneath my armpits grasping me tightly, and then I was being yanked upward.

"I got you."

I looked up.

Now, diner light is hardly flattering, but it hit Dean's face in a surprisingly dramatic way. His eyes were wide, shocked, and searching my face in what I quickly realized was frantic concern. His uniform was rumpled at the collar, shadows cast against his sharp features... cheesy, I know, but at that moment, it was like I'd forgotten how darn handsome he was.

Dean tugged me to the side of the kitchen and set me on my feet. I was so taken aback; I didn't even have time to think about the fact that Dean was now in the same room as the creature—a creature with tusks, and bristles all over its pink skin. I was spared in having to decide how in the world I was going to explain this to Dean as he then lifted his hand and drew a pistol from the holster at his waist. Then he aimed that pistol on the hog-man that was now barreling around the prep counter and coming right at us.

"What in the fuck is that!" Dean managed as he then turned his face to me. "Twila, run, now!" he shouted, and then fired two shots.

The bullets missed the hog-man, but the shifter squealed anyway and scurried off in the other direction, driven away from its course for a moment. And that was when my sense came flooding back to me: if I let Dean put himself between me and this thing, he was going to get hurt. Or worse because the hog-man was a shifter of some kind, and there was no way a human could go up against a shifter and win.

So, even with my injured ankle and knee, I ran.

But, not for the back door, which I'm sure was what Dean had meant. Instead, I rushed to the far side of the kitchen and yanked open the utility closet. Glancing back, I noticed the beast was staggering, the sound of the gunshots having startled it, and that pause gave me just enough time to grab a solid wood broom and sprint back. I was just in time, too, because the hog-man pounced at the same time that Dean fired his gun, lodging a bullet right in the thing's rib cage.

With the force of the bullets, the thing flew past me and smacked into the wall. It made an animalistic squeal of pain as it fell to the ground. But, not taking any chances, I came up on it and swung the broomstick in its face, catching it mid-arc. Instantly, I heard the sound of wood and bone *cracking* and with a pitiful whimpering noise, the hog-man clutched its obviously broken nose and scuttled right back towards the rear wall of the kitchen, cowering in obvious submission as it backed through the opening in the door.

I heard Dean cock the gun again and felt the broom drop to the ground as my head started to pound. I felt woozy; the adrenaline forcing me into a state of oxygen over-exposure. This had happened once before—when I'd pushed myself too hard in another case when we'd corralled a centaur.

"It's not going to attack again," I said, not wanting Dean to kill the thing—not when we still didn't know who it was. I'd have to get the boys to go after it later. It was obviously injured and needed medical attention. For now, though, I had to figure out what in the world to tell Dean.

"What in the hell was it?" Dean asked, staring at the opening in the door where the thing had pushed through, no doubt disappearing into the woods behind the diner. As Dean pushed against the door, he kept his gun at low-ready in front of him.

That was a question I didn't even know how to begin to answer and at the thought, the pounding in my head increased in intensity. Leaning against the wall, I fought to catch my breath and turned to survey the damage surrounding me. I cursed under my breath as I wished I hadn't sent Hannah after the Dooleys.

Now, I had *two* messes to clean up.

Not to mention the mess known as 'Dean just witnessed a shifter trying to kill me'.

***

Dean tore off a strip of medical tape and placed it over the gauze he'd already put on my knee, shooting me a pitiful glance as I hissed at the burning spark that shot through my leg. Deputy Drayton had left a while ago, searching the forest for any clues as to where the intruder might have gone, and for any other patrons who might have been scared off by the attack. So far, he'd located the cook, Hal, and taken down his account (being careful to omit exactly what the thing had looked like). We closed the diner for the day—the kitchen in no shape to continue operating.

Now, it was just Dean and me, with Dean kneeling in front of me as I propped my leg up on a barstool. I kept looking down at him, waiting for him to bring up the inevitable. Yet, he remained focused on the task at hand. When he'd finished bandaging up my knee, he stood up and lifted my other leg, brushing his fingers over my shin, where a blob of flour had left a powdery spot. I couldn't help the fact that my skin washed over with goosebumps as soon as he dragged his fingertips across it. And, yes, I was more than aware that he could feel the intensity of the heat of my skin, but he wasn't commenting so neither was I.

He dropped my leg and then lifted my arm, clearly attempting to search every part of me for more cuts and bruises, and just like with my legs, my arms were covered in gooseflesh as soon as he finished inspecting them.

Dean had always been gentle, even back in high school. Gentle touches, gentle words, gentle smiles across the school hallways, gentle kisses underneath the bleachers. And the first time he'd introduced me to the joys between a man and a woman, he'd been the gentlest. Thinking about that now, I felt my internal temperature increase and cleared my throat in spite of myself. Yes, there had been enough men since Dean but it's true what they say—you never do forget your first.

"I think you're okay, Twila," he said in that deep, raspy voice of his that caused me to swallow hard.

There had always been something about Dean—maybe it was the way he spoke so slowly and with such authority, or maybe it was the fact that he was always scanning his surroundings, always one step ahead of any and everyone around him. Whatever it was—I'd always felt safe with him. And I felt that way now too.

"It makes sense that you found your way into law enforcement," I said, momentarily taking him aback—proof enough in the surprise that echoed in his raised brows. "That—well, that's just the sort of personality you have."

"I suppose... so," he answered and gave me a polite smile—one that said his mind wasn't contemplating just why he'd ended up as a sheriff.

But I was thinking about just that—maybe because I didn't want to have to consider alternative conversations because I knew there was only *one* alternative conversation we were going to have. And I was in no rush to have it. So, I just focused on sitting there beside him, and I focused on how familiar it felt. It was just like it always had been—Dean making sure I was safe and sound against whatever went bump in the dark. Now, though, I was unfortunately the *exact* thing that went bump in the dark.

Not finding that line of thinking consoling, I thought back to the last time we'd spent quality, alone time together—when Dean had turned eighteen and I was barely seventeen. We'd driven up to Snowy Peak Mountain with the express purpose of watching the sun set. And when we'd sat on that ledge, overlooking the splendor of the mighty Ozarks as the dying sun set the sky ablaze with a vibrant gradient of orange and violet, I'd thought to myself how perfect everything was—how lucky I was to be so in love with such a wonderful man and to have the love of that wonderful man in return. Yes, it had been perfect, right until the moment our eyes met and Dean told me he was leaving Windy Ridge. And then my life started to shatter right in front of me.

He'd wanted me to come with him.

"We could get married," he'd said. *"Start over somewhere new, Twila. Leave this town behind. Just you and me. We could travel the world, just like you always wanted."*

And he was right. I *had* always wanted exactly that. For years, I'd told him about my dreams to see the world, to understand what I'd been missing all these years I'd been stuck in Windy Ridge.

But even though Dean's plan sounded so romantic and incredible, I'd been scared. As scared as any remotely sensible teenager would have been in a similar situation. My GPA was barely passing, and Dean only had a thousand dollars to his name. I was too young to recognize a get-out-of-jail-free-card when I saw one and, instead, I'd worried I'd be throwing what little future I had away. So, after dashing his hopes with a handful of words I only barely managed to bring beyond my lips, Dean drove me home.

And every day since, I regretted that decision.

I did end up moving to Branson eventually, but it was a year later and I didn't have many hopes of actually finding Dean, even though word was that Branson was exactly where he'd ended up. Regardless, I settled in and found love again, but it was never the same *kind* of love. The kind of love Dean and I had shared was the type of innocent love you dream of as a little girl—the *soul* type of love that grabs you and won't let go. To this day, I considered myself very lucky to have ever experienced that sort of love—even if I'd only ever found it in my adolescence.

Yes, there was something about Dean that had been different back then. I'd never quite known what that thing was but the more men I'd met and dated, the more I'd realized Dean was a different sort—cut from a completely different bolt of fabric. And though I regretted allowing him to slip through my fingers, eventually I forced myself to stop thinking about him, to stop wondering where I would have been if I'd taken him up on his offer. Where *we* would have been. Instead, I pushed the memories of those years away and settled into being a single mother, living a life I hadn't planned for but was making the best of.

Chapter Eight

"Thanks, Dean," I managed, suddenly finding the quiet between us unbearable.

After what had just happened, what we'd both experienced, it should have been anything but quiet between us.

He nodded, and then just looked at me, and I just looked at him. And neither of us said anything for what felt like minutes, but was probably more like three to five seconds.

"You're right quiet," he said finally.

I nodded. "So are you."

It was his turn to nod. "So, I am."

I watched him stand and there was something so sexy about the movement—how slow it was, yet how predatory. Of course, the irony of that thought wasn't lost on me—of the two of us, I was obviously the predator and yet... yet there was something in those dark and narrowed eyes, something in the deadly lines of his jaw that was somehow threatening... and even more so, sexually stimulating.

By the grace of God, what in the world has gotten into me, I thought to myself, completely and totally shocked by these feelings that had been flowing through me ever since Dean had shown up in Windy Ridge. In general, I was a calm, level-headed, unemotional woman and yet... where those respectable traits had disappeared to was anyone's question.

I glanced up at Dean, where he was now towering over me. His eyes scanned my face and arms, as though still searching for any sign of injury, and from the way his hands kept twitching at his sides, I couldn't help but think he wanted to keep touching me.

And darn it all but I *wanted* him to keep touching me.

"You think you're hurt any place else?" he asked.

"I... don't think so," I answered as I rubbed the back of my head, touching a sore spot where I'd smacked it against the counter. "Nothing you can patch up, at least."

My wounds were going to be healed within the hour, but there was no need to tell him that. Keeping up this charade would take a lot from me, I thought.

"You sure?" He pursed his lips, unconvinced and shifted his weight from one leg to the other.

That was when I noticed he had a slightly bow-legged stance—like he was a cowboy who'd just come in from rounding up his cattle.

Cowboy? Cattle? I inwardly shook my head. I was embarrassed for myself.

"You took a bit of a beating," he continued, looking at me in that caring way of his.

"Yeah," I answered, thinking maybe that beating was the reason my emotions were all over the place. I laughed slightly then, though I wasn't sure why, and the jolt of my muscles made my stomach churn. With the mixture of sunlight, fatigue, and the stress on my body, it was like the worst hangover I'd ever had. I was getting more nauseous by the minute, but I did my best to hide it. With my luck, Dean would try and drag me to the nearest hospital, and that was miles away. Who knew what they would find if they put me in an MRI?

"If I'd taken the same beating, I might doubt what I'm pretty sure I just saw."

And the butterflies were back in my stomach and then some. Actually, these were more like angry crows who were dive-bombing each other.

I looked up at him and found his gaze riveted to my face. His jaw was tight and his eyes dared me to lie to him.

"What... what did you think you saw?"

"A man."

"Oh," I started, frowning, but Dean interrupted.

"With the pinkest skin I ever saw... and tusks growing out of his jaw."

I laughed. I didn't know what else to do. Dean's

frown grew.

"I... uh, I didn't see that," I answered, even though I felt all kinds of guilty for doing so.

"You didn't?" He switched his weight to the other foot again.

I shook my head. "In case you didn't notice, I was basically fighting for my life," I managed as I breathed in a deep breath. "But obviously it wasn't a pink man with tusks," I continued as I gave him a smile that said there was nothing to worry about. "I'm sure it was just some... meth-head, wearing a mask so we wouldn't be able to see his face."

"It didn't look like a mask."

I swallowed hard. "Deputy Drayton—"

"Said he hasn't seen anything," Dean interrupted as he reached down and offered me his hand. I took it and he yanked me up to my feet. "I shot the thing right in the chest," he continued, shaking his head. "It didn't look like taking a bullet fazed him at *all.*"

"You know what they say about drug addicts—sometimes they have super-human strength."

"Right." But he didn't sound convinced.

For a moment, I caught his eyes again and was surprised by what I saw there. His expression wasn't doubting, necessarily, but I was familiar enough with interrogation methods from my investigations to know a searching look when I saw one. And that's the exact expression Dean was giving me —a searching one. For some reason, I felt my heart clench. It... *hurt* to see him doubting me, which was ironic, considering I'd just gotten done lying to his face. It wasn't even that I disliked being doubted, but Dean doubting me specifically? Yeah, *Dean* doubting me made me feel like there was a hole inside my chest.

And that was just plain stupid because Dean and me... we weren't anything. And we'd continue being nothing.

"I want to ask you a favor," Dean said and my heart further plummeted.

"What kind of favor?"

"Remember my nephew, Mason?"

"Of course."

He nodded. "He's a sketch artist."

"Okay."

He nodded again. "If you're up to it, it would be helpful if you'd come with me to the station and work with Mason to get a drawing of the suspect."

"But I... I didn't get a good look at him."

"Anything would help."

I laughed, but the sound was a concerned one. "I think you saw him better than I did."

"And I'll have my time with Mason, but first I'd like for you to have yours."

For a moment, I hesitated.

I felt like unleashing hell on the Dooley house for putting this mess on my doorstep in the first place, but then I realized that wasn't really why I was so upset. What was causing my unrest was the fact that I couldn't be honest with Dean and, what was more, he knew I wasn't being honest with him.

Regardless, now there was only one decision to be made—I had to go to the station with him. Refuse and I'd look even more suspicious. Either way, I had to play along, no matter what.

There was a buzzing in my pocket and I pulled out my cell phone. Checking the caller ID, I sighed when I saw Sicily's name and photo pop up on the screen.

"Sorry, I have to take this," I said to Dean who just nodded at me. Stepping a few paces away from him, I answered. "Hey, honey—"

"Mama, are you okay?!" Sicily's voice was panicked, and from her sharp intakes of breath, I could tell she was running or walking very fast. "I got a call from Stacy—"

"Stacy?" I couldn't think enough to place whoever Sicily was talking about.

"Chameleon?"

"Oh, right, *that* Stacy."

"Right—anyway, she said you just got attacked."

I cringed. Now that I thought about it, Stacy had been inside the diner when all the ruckus had started in the back. So, of course she would have told Sicily. Privacy wasn't a thing in small towns, and that was *especially* true for this one.

"Mama?" Sicily demanded, her voice breaking.

"I'm okay, I'm okay."

"Are you just doing what moms do and pretending everything is okay?"

"No, I'm fine. I promise. Just a few scratches, that's all."

"So, there *was* an attack?!"

"Well, yeah," I started and then Sicily's tone changed to one of excitement.

"Was it the shifter?"

"I—" Quietly, I side-eyed Dean, worried he could overhear my conversation, but he was still a good distance away, even if his eyes were locked on me from that distance. "—um, I can't really talk at the moment, Sicily. I'm with the sheriff and I've got to go down to the station for a little bit."

"Are you... in trouble?"

"No," I answered on a laugh. "I'll be home in a few hours."

"Okay, Mama. You sure you're okay?"

"I promise, everything's okay."

Sicily paused, and it was like I could *hear* her mind working from over the receiver. "Trying not to appear suspicious, okay, got it. I'll meet you at the station so I can back you up if you need it."

"Wh—" I checked my watch. "Sicily, you're supposed to be in school."

"Stacy called me in the middle of English and I excused myself due to a family emergency." I could hear the pride in her voice and the humor of it all almost squashed the anger that flared inside me. Still, her stubbornness didn't seem to help much with my headache at the moment.

"Are you *walking* all the way from Dagwood?"

"Of course not! Boone picked me up."

Ugh, that man was going to cause the death of

me. "*Sicily—*"

"See you at the station!"

Click. The phone went dead, and I had to bite down on my tongue to keep myself from unleashing a slew of curses in front of the sheriff.

"Everything okay?" he asked.

I nodded. "Sicily, my daughter, just informed me she's on her way to your station."

"Why?"

I shook my head. "Because wherever the action is, she wants to be in the center of it."

When I turned to face him, he was pressing his lips together tightly, holding in a laugh, and I scowled as I stepped back over to him.

"…That girl of yours seems to have a determined head on her shoulders," he said, hands in his pockets in an infuriatingly cocky way.

"Determined to be in everyone else's business," I answered on a sigh.

Dean smiled, the apparent distrust now vacant in his gaze. "I'm happy I'll get the chance to meet her."

"Let's see if you're still singing that song after you do," I answered on a smile.

He just grinned at me and motioned for us to leave.

***

The ride up to Windy Hill was quiet. As to the

influx of nausea I'd felt once I had to step back into the sunlight, it was still present and accounted for. I must have looked as bad as I felt because I kept catching Dean looking at me while he drove his sheriff-issued Ford Explorer.

"I'm okay," I said after the nth glance.

"You don't look so good."

Maybe that was because I'd spent most of the ride with my eyes shut, breathing deeply until we arrived at the Windy Ridge station, an old building made of brick and concrete.

"I'll be fine."

"Maybe I should get you to a hospital."

I looked over at him. "No hospital. I'm fine. My nerves are just a mess, that's all."

He studied me for a few more seconds before Sicily spotted us and came running over, Boone standing outside his jalopy of a vehicle. I'd never been happier to see my daughter.

I got out of Dean's cruiser as Sicily reached me, throwing her arms around me.

"You had me so worried."

"I'm fine, Sicily."

She gave me a smile, then turned to face Dean. "And this must be our new sheriff!"

And then she was flitting away from me and starting towards him.

"Sicily, I presume?" Dean asked as he offered her a big smile.

"I am," she answered with a big grin and a strange sort of curtsey like she thought she was meeting the queen.

"You've got your mama's spunk," Dean said as he extended his hand and Sicily took it. "I'm Dean. I'm glad to finally meet you."

"I'm glad to finally meet you," Sicily answered and by the way she was smiling at him, I could tell she thought he was cute. Oh, brother.

Then she abruptly turned on her toes and was already making her way to the concrete front steps. She turned to face us and plopped her hands on her hips.

"Well, what are you waiting for?" Then she glanced over at Boone, before facing me again. "Can Boone come too?"

I looked at Dean. "Can Boone come too?"

Dean smiled as he inhaled deeply and exhaled just as deeply—like he wasn't used to this sort of thing when he worked law enforcement in Branson. "He's already here," he answered with a little nod. "It's like it's become a field trip."

"Come on, Boone," Sicily called to him and he pushed off from where he was leaning against his rusted-out wreck that had once been a 1986 AMC Eagle but now had so many borrowed parts that it looked more like something a kid in third grade drew.

Dean bypassed Sicily and then opened one of the double doors to the station and allowed all of us to enter. Dean led us through the empty lobby, and down one of the corridors. The walls were gray, plain, and from the lack of noise, I had to wonder if they'd been insulated with some kind of noise-canceling foam or something. Not that I minded. Some peace and quiet was just what I and my headache needed at the moment.

Dean then paused on his march down the hallway and opening one of the doors, poked his head inside. "Hey, Mason. Are you busy?"

"Hmm?" A muffled, youthful voice replied, and there was a flutter of what sounded like stiff paper in reply. "Uh, no, not really. Just organizing. Why?"

Dean stepped back and gave us a nod, and we walked inside to see a messy office space with three well-used desks in the corners, though only one was currently occupied.

Mason Hawke was seated around a pile of documents, a red mark on his lower jaw that hinted to the fact that he'd been resting his hand on it for quite a while. He raised a brow as we entered, looking to his uncle with a question in his eyes.

"This is Twila Boseman—you remember her from the diner?"

Mason faced me and smiled. "Oh, yeah, of course. Nice to see you again, Ms. Boseman."

"Please, call me Twila," I answered with a smile. "And it's nice to see you again too, Mason."

"And this is Twila's daughter, Sicily," Dean said and gestured to the young miss in question. As I glanced at Sicily and then at Mason, I realized that both of them were looking at the other with undisguised admiration.

Great, just great.

"And don't forget Boone," Sicily said as she

reached around, gripping Boone around the wrist and yanking him forward so hard, I was surprised she didn't free his arm from its socket.

"I'm B-B-Boone."

Mason extended his hand. "I'm Mason, nice to meet you."

Then Mason faced Dean again, the same question in his eyes.

"Twila was attacked by someone recently at the diner and I'd like you to talk to her so we can hopefully get a sketch down of the suspect."

Mason's eyes lit up and at once, he was on his feet, a few papers fluttering down around him. "Absolutely. Just gimmie one sec." Then he looked at me and frowned. "Sorry, I was alphabetizing and stuff."

I chuckled slightly and glanced at my daughter who was staring at Mason like she'd never seen a cute boy before. I looked back at the young man and smiled. "Take your time. Like I told your uncle —I didn't really get a good look at the guy so I'm not sure how much help I'll be."

And I was definitely not going to bring up the shifter's pink skin, the wiry bristles all over his body and the tusks from his underslung jaw. And that meant—I wasn't going to be any help at all.

Mason flashed me a shy smile, and he started to gather up his documents as Dean led us to a small table in an adjoining room. I could see a few stray documents lying on the table top and glancing at them, they appeared to be landscapes and sketches of various wild animals, all done in a quick-stroked, yet detailed manner. The signature on the corners solidified my suspicions: *M. Hawke.*

Sicily walked up beside me, and when she glanced down and saw the drawings, she turned around, looking at Mason as he grabbed a stack of papers and a pencil case from the desk.

"Did you draw all of these?"

"Huh?" Mason paused, and then his eyes fell to the numerous drawings on the table. "Oh, yeah. I forgot I left those there—was just warming up this morning, and I forgot to put them away, let me just —"

"Warming up?" Sicily nearly choked on her own words. "Mason, these are *amazing.*" She reached out and grabbed the page Mason was about to snatch away, holding it hostage with a victorious smile. "No wonder you got this gig. Your linework is great."

That seemed to throw him off and, as I watched, his cheeks colored every shade of red.

Dean snickered as his nephew awkwardly stood beside him, brushing hair out of his eyes and making it stick up the sides of his head.

"Oh. Uh, thanks." Mason flashed Sicily a little smile, one that looked almost *exactly* like his uncle's, and then turned to me. "Um, I'm ready for you, now, Miss Twila. You can take a seat wherever you want."

***

The sketching session was blissfully short, all told. Mason was fast, and it didn't take us long to get into a flow, though I did have to choose my words carefully, explaining all of the human traits of the man that had attacked me without mentioning the monstrous bits.

Together, we managed to make something of a portrayal (decidedly without the tusks) of the shifter's human side, and I was even allowed to take a picture so I could show the boys later on (not that I told the Hawkes that). Once we were all done, Dean insisted on taking me home so we didn't have to trudge our way back down the hillside myself (or drive with Boone and given how much trash was all over his vehicle, I would have rather walked home). Boone was under strict orders to get Sicily back to school.

"Thanks for the ride," I said to Dean as I turned to face him and took a step back when I found him standing right in front of me.

He pressed his hand to my shoulder. "Hey, hang on a second."

I paused and tried to hope nothing bad was going to come out of his mouth. All the while, I noticed he was chewing the inside of his cheek—the same thing he'd done as a young man when he was facing some kind of obstacle. This was the first time I'd seen Dean wearing a shred of anxiety.

"Are you... sure you're gonna be okay, er, safe

here Twila?"

"Um," I started.

"I mean—whoever that attacker was back at the diner—is there any chance he knows you personally?"

"Like did he have it out for me or something?"

"Sure," Dean nodded.

I laughed as I shook my head. "No, Dean, he didn't. It was just a random meth addict looking for something to eat." But the words rang false as soon as I said them. And Dean noticed, I was sure, because he nodded really quickly and took a step back, dropping his hold of my shoulder.

I smiled, though I knew it didn't meet my eyes. "Thanks for all your help, Dean. I mean it." Then I breathed in really big and deep as I remembered the mess still waiting for me at the diner. The last thing I wanted was for Dorcas to show up before I had it cleaned up. "Anyway, I've gotta get back and clean up the diner, but, uh..." I tried to give him a better smile. "See you around?"

Dean nodded. "Yeah," I heard him say as I turned back to the walkway that cut through the woods and led to the diner. "I can drive you, Twila."

"I'm fine," I called back as I waved my hand and didn't bother to turn around.

Chapter Nine

"I'LL HUNT THAT NO-GOOD, ROTTEN, SUMMA-BITCH DOWN MYSELF!"

Dorcas had been screaming for the last hour, though this time, not at me. As luck would have it, when I got back to the diner, she'd already arrived. And, word on the street was (aka from Hannah) that when Dorcas saw the mess the shifter left in the kitchen, anyone within a half-block could have heard her bellowing.

It took a solid ten minutes for her to even register that I'd arrived, she was so mad. I couldn't really blame her. The shifter had gone through about half of our stock of food, knocked over things, banged into others until the entire kitchen looked like the setting for a disaster movie.

When I showed her my (nearly healed) injuries, she took a bit of pity on me and allowed me to sit while I started washing the dishes. The trade-off, of course, was that I had to listen to her shout-complaints as she cleaned up the rest of the kitchen herself. Hannah, meanwhile, tended to anyone who showed up in the front—we were now open for business again, but only for coffee, donuts and whatever else hadn't been destroyed by the shifter.

"WHEN YOU FIND OUT WHO THIS DADGUM RAT-BASTARD IS, I'M GONNA TAN HIS HIDE SO BROWN, YOU CAN MAKE BOOTS FROM IT." Dorcas' head was shoved inside the refrigerator while she cleaned it out, so her voice was echoing off the tight walls until she sort of sounded like Darth Vader. "NO EGGS, NO GREENS, NO 'MATERS, NO 'TATERS, NO BEEF, NO SPAGHETTI—I SWEAR, KIDS LIKE YOU AIN'T RIGHT IN THE HEAD."

My head was still throbbing from what I'd termed 'sunlight sickness', so I didn't respond. I just sat there, quietly washing the dishes that hadn't been shattered in the attack, until Dorcas' mole head popped out of the fridge and stared at me.

"WHAT DID THAT THING LOOK LIKE, ANYWAYS?" She asked, and the sound waves rattled my brain so much, I nearly yelped out in pain. Instead, I turned on my stool and put my hands on the side of my face, fingers splayed to look like bristles, and then curled my index fingers around my bottom lip to mimic tusks.

"A WALRUS?" Dorcas shouted. "WE GOT ATTACKED BY A HILLBILLY WALRUS? WHAT IN TARNATION?"

I sighed, then shook my head and wiggled my

hands and pointed to my feet.

"WE GOT ATTACKED BY A WALRUS WITH FEET? WEARING HEELS?"

I shook my head and I'm sure I looked as flustered as I felt. Then I pushed the tip of my nose down so it flattened out some.

"A WALRUS THAT LOOKED LIKE A HOG," she said, and I snapped my fingers and nodded. "WE GOT OURSELVES A DANG HOG-MAN 'ROUND HERE NOW? GOSHDARN IT, I SWEAR, THIS TOWN NEVER GETS ANY EASIER."

I shrugged, though I did agree with her. You would think after a few months, even the craziest of situations would calm down. But not around Windy Ridge, apparently. My little charade game reminded me of the picture I'd taken on my phone, and while I had Dorcas' attention, I stood and clicked open the gallery, pressing the sketch Mason had drawn in front of Dorcas' face. She squinted at it, her beady little mole eyes clearly having trouble seeing it.

"...WHOZZAT?" She asked finally, and again, my skull rang with the volume of her voice. I stepped back and did the motions again, flat nose, bristles, tusks coming from the thing's lips. Then, I pointed at the picture again, brows raised in a rendition of: *Ever seen him before?*

"NO, HE DON'T LOOK NONE FAMILIAR AND HE DEFINITELY DON'T LOOK LIKE NO WALRUS."

I grabbed a pad of paper and immediately wrote down: *Not walrus. Hog.*

"OH, THAT'S RIGHT. I DONE GOT MY TUSKS MIXED UP. HOG-MAN." Dorcas sniffed, her whiskers waving in the breeze. "AIN'T FROM HERE, PROBL'Y NOT FROM DAGWOOD, NEITHER. DEVIL'S RUN, IF I HAD TO GUESS. THEM'S FOLKS ALWAYS CAUSIN' TROUBLE. I BET IT WAS SOMEONE TRYIN' TO RUIN MY BUSINESS, RUN ME OUT DRY BY EATIN' ALL MY VITTLES. WHY, THE LAST TIME I WENT THERE, I—"

But I'd already walked away from Dorcas before her voice could send me into a coma and I returned to my post at the sink, where I sped through the rest of the dishes. I was exhausted, the last forty-eight hours showing themselves with a bite as mean as a hound's, and all I wanted to do was get back to my trailer and sleep until Sicily came home from school. Granted, I didn't need much sleep, but I needed some now. After everything I'd been through, my body was feeling it.

And if Dorcas didn't know anything about our shifter, that meant I had nothing more to do here, so I grabbed my notepad, writing a quick *I need to go or else you'll have to pay me overtime* message on it and held it up to her face real close like.

"BEAT IT, GIRL. I AIN'T MADE O' MONEY NO WAY, NO HOW."

That was enough for me and before long, I was rushing out the door. At this point, the sunlight was *preferable* to remaining in Dorcas' presence any longer.

Once I was back on the path that led to River's Edge Trailer Park, my own trailer felt like it was a lifetime away. Even equipped with my protective clothing, I felt like I was going to collapse with every step I took. Not to mention, I kept looking over my shoulder whenever something rustled in the underbrush. Most of the time I was alert, sure, but the shifter attack had gotten me downright *jumpy*. I was half-convinced that, if it *did* ambush me again, I'd be so fed up, I might accidentally kill the thing before anyone could come and help. Thankfully, though, nothing launched itself at me as I wandered my way home. At last, I could get in my bed, curl up under the covers and pretend this whole mess was just a bad dream, at least for a little while.

I opened my trailer door and almost in reflex, my jacket fell off my shoulders, a breath of relief leaving my throat. I threw the heavy thing onto the coat rack along with my sunglasses then shut the door behind me as I kicked off my shoes, groaning while I reached behind me to unzip my uniform. Glancing at Sicily, who was seated on the couch, I gave her a smile.

"Hey, Sicily," I mumbled as I stumbled past her, on my way towards my bed. The covers looked so inviting, our black-out curtains keeping any trace of sunlight from peeking inside. It may not have been much, but to me, it looked like paradise after the day I'd had.

But then I stopped.

Because Sicily was *not* supposed to be home. She was supposed to be at school, where she was supposed to have been dropped off by Boone.

I turned on my heel, my focus suddenly razor-sharp.

Sicily, meanwhile, was staring at me wide-eyed from her seat on the couch, but I quickly realized she wasn't the only one inside. Nope—the empty beer cans that were sitting on the table were evidence enough. And not a second later, the door opened and Bud, Ol' Ned, and Boone walked in together. As soon as Bud saw me, he frantically leapt for the tabletop, sweeping papers off the surface with his werewolf mitt-hands and into a large bag that I recognized as Bud's suitcase of evidence.

"Well, what do you three have to say for yourselves?" I demanded, while plopping my hands on my hips and glaring at all three of them in turn.

Every single one of them looked like guilty schoolchildren; Boone's large eyes were darting back and forth, Ol' Ned's lizard tongue flicked anxiously out of his mouth, and Bud's ears flattened against his skull, head sinking pitifully in between his shoulders.

"... You have *got,*" I started as I stepped forward. I could have sworn that every single person in the trailer jumped and scurried back when I did, "to be *kidding* me."

"Hey, Mama." Sicily raised her hand in a half-wave, smiling nervously. "Um. I'm home."

I looked at Boone. "You didn't take her back to

school, did you?"

Boone swallowed hard. I took another step forward.

"Boone, I swear to God, you better answer me. *Now.*"

"... I-I-I'm sorry, Miss T-T-Twila," he stuttered, and both Bud and Ol' Ned groaned in defeat. "She—well, sh-she was right insistful that I—"

"I do not *care* what she insisted! You *do not* get to decide when my child skips school!" Then I looked at the others. "And you two are just as bad!"

While some parents had to grow out of their mama voice when their children got older, I pulled it out every now and again when I needed Bud and the others to listen, and now was certainly one of those times.

"I'm r-r-right sorry, Miss T-T-Twila," Boone started, his stutter more pronounced. But I was having none of it.

"What kind o' a circus do you think I'm runnin', here? Need I remind you that Sicily is *not* your child? An' she *isn't* your little *protégé,* either!" That sentence I directed at Bud, whose tail was fully between his legs now and pretty soon he'd probably start whimpering. "You're gonna go behind my back and disrespect my authority regardin' my own kid? Is *that* how we're gonna play this game?"

None of them answered, not even Sicily, who was looking much angrier than the others.

"The answer's 'no'!" I yelled at them. "I'm not

gonna let my only daughter rot in this shitbox town! She's smart—smarter than any o' us and she don't deserve to get stuck here for the rest o' her life!"

I marched back over to the door and wrenched it open, letting the handle slam fully into the wall behind it as Bud cried and his ears dropped as low as they'd go. "Get outta my trailer, all of you! I don't wanna see hide nor hair of any o' your sorry asses for at least a few days, an' that's *if* I decide I wanna see'em ever again!"

I pointed to the door. The boys glanced at each other for a moment before they turned around, heads hung in pitiful regret as they marched single-file through the door, onto the porch, down the stairs and onto the road outside my trailer. Then I let the door fall shut, making sure they could hear the *clank* of it hitting the frame, and let my breath hiss out of my tightened lungs. After which I turned and faced Sicily, who was glaring at me.

"You didn't have to *scream* at them like that." She had her arms folded, her messy brown hair hardly covering the fury on her face.

I scoffed and raised my eyebrows. "They're not your parents, Sicily. I can't *believe* you used them to get out of class."

"I didn't use them to get out of class, Mama! I wanted to help with the shifter case!"

"Sicily," I started, but she shook her head and gave me her best 'insistent' stare.

"There's normies like *me* in town, now, Mama, so you know this thing has to be caught as quickly as possible. It *attacked* you, right in front of Dean and you know he saw it!"

That made me pause. Sicily looked genuinely worried, and I felt a surge of guilt wash over me that I quickly tried to push down again as I remembered where she should have been. "I took care of it. I'm stronger than anything in this town, and you know that."

"That's not the *point!* You can still get hurt, can't you? And the longer this thing is out there, runnin' around, the more likely a normie's gonna see it! Or get killed by it! Why can't you just let me help?!"

"Sicily," I gave a frustrated huff and rubbed my temples where my headache now felt like my head was imploding on my brain and my brain wasn't having none of it. "I *told* you why you can't be cuttin' class for this damn paranormal crap."

"And it *still* doesn't make any sense!" Sicily shouted and spread her arms out wide, gesturing to the few stacks of papers and books she and the rest of the boys had been looking at. The pages of notes were rumpled and the text small, so as much information could be packed on one page as possible. "The guys don't know how to do research, Mama. They don't know how to work a smartphone, let alone search the internet forums for actual cases of shifters an' monster appearances. I'm the *only one* who can get the information we need!"

"That doesn't mean you should be skipping school, Sicily!" I stepped up towards her, feeling the heat of my body and the heat of her anger clashing in the air between us. "I'm just trying to give you a chance to have a *future!"*

Sicily straightened up. Then she looked me dead in the eye, a reflection of my own anger on her face. "What you want is for me to build my skills, right? To go to school and explore my interests and use them?" I nodded. "Well, I've aced Biology for the past three and a half years and now I'm using it to figure out how everyone's bodies have changed. AP Chemistry has helped me to come up with my own tests so I can try to figure some of this stuff out. History, Literature, Art, Psychology—I'm using *all those subjects* to help the team." She took a deep, deep breath. "You want me to have a future, right? *This* is my future, Mama. Helping this town, figuring out what's going on with that fog, understanding what the fog was—that is the future I want!"

"This isn't a *future*, Sicily! Windy Ridge is a dead-end town in the middle of the mountains, out in the middle of nowhere, USA. You can't expect to go anywhere if you end up stuck here all your life."

"Leaving this place was your dream, Mama, but it's not mine. I care about this town and the people in it and I want to do everything I can to help them!"

My head was now pounding in earnest and I couldn't stand the thought of one more argumentative statement passing between the two of us. Pressing my palms over my eyes, I felt my teeth grate against each other with the tightening of my jaw. "I'm done, I am *done* talking about this with you.

Go to your room, and if you're out before sunset, you're losing technology rights for a week. *Understand?"*

I faced her again. Her cheeks were red, eyes bulging with obvious rage, and I could see her hands balled and shaking by her sides. I stared her down until she stalked off, giving me one last, venomous look with her hand on the door.

"… You need to ask yourself if it's right to push your wants and dreams on me."

With that, the door slammed. The tension in the air released. I deflated, sinking onto the couch cushions, blocking any light with the heels of my hands. Everything between my eyes throbbed and it was all I could do to take in a deep breath.

It was then that I felt my phone buzz from inside my apron pocket.

At this point, if it was one of the boys, I was gonna throw it at the wall. But it wasn't—in fact, it was a phone number I didn't recognize. Shakily, I clicked the answer button, slowly pressing the speaker up to my ear.

"… Hello?"

"Hey, Twila," said my ex, Alton, the smile on his face visible in his voice. "I hope you're well."

"I, uh, I'm okay," I answered.

There was a quick pause. "Well, I'm just calling to chat with Sicily…"

At the idea of facing my daughter, if only to tell her to talk to her pa, I recoiled a little on the inside.

Chapter Ten

It had been a while since I'd talked to Alton.

And that was usually intentional. While we may have been on good terms, I knew it was difficult to talk to an ex you still had feelings for and Alton had told me as much about a year ago, before Sicily stopped contacting him. He was also surprisingly accepting of the fact that I couldn't reciprocate those feelings. That hope had fizzled out a long time ago for me, and even though Alton was notably disappointed, he never tried to make me feel bad about it. As far as I knew, he'd just accepted it and moved on.

As to why my feelings couldn't rekindle themselves? I wasn't entirely sure. Alton was a handsome enough man, and he was smart and kind. Yet, whenever I thought about getting back together with him, all I could remember was the hell his parents had put him through regarding dating me and then having a child with me. And that was enough. I was just glad and grateful that Alton wanted to be an active member of Sicily's life. Most men in my experience didn't seem to care about their 'oops' baby, especially not rich ones.

Still, hearing Alton's voice now was jarring, especially considering the day I'd had. I was struck with stunned silence until I heard him clear his throat, a slight pause tailing behind his voice.

"Twila? You still there?" His voice, contrary to Dean's or Bud's or anyone else's in the Ozarks, was crisp, cheerful, and without an accent. And Alton always sounded younger than he really was.

"Yeah, yeah, sorry. I'm still here." I squeezed my eyes shut and forced the lump of stress out of my throat so I could talk.

"You get my check I sent?" he asked. Alton was good about paying child support and he paid right on time, every month, so he was more than aware that I'd received his check.

"I did. Thank you."

"Hey… it's… it's good to hear you."

"It's good to hear your voice too." I laughed, though I wasn't sure why. "I, uh, I didn't mean to space out just now. I'm just not feeling great right now."

"Oh… I'm sorry to hear that." He sounded just as uncomfortable as I was sure I did. But, not wanting to focus on things I couldn't help, I instead focused on the fact that I could hear birds in the background and wondered if he was by the coast, trekking off on some vacation again.

"Is there anything I can help out with, maybe?" he continued and there was a hopeful tone to his voice. "I have a really good doctor referral I could give you."

"Oh, no, thank you," I said tiredly even as the thought of a human doctor sent a shiver down my spine. "It's just a cold, I think. I'll be okay."

"Alright, if you're sure."

"I am."

Pause. "What's, uh, what's been going on lately?"

"Oh, you know." I nearly laughed again as I crossed my legs and still had no idea what in the world I found so funny. "More of the same."

"Dorcas still giving you grief?" It was his turn to laugh.

"Ha, you don't know the half of it."

The smile was still in his voice when he responded, "you know she only gives you a hard time because you're her best server. She's probably just jealous!"

"Aside from Hannah, who's part-time, I'm her *only* server, Alton." I *did* smirk at his compliment, though. "What about you? Where are you stationed today?"

"Oh, I'm back in Branson, actually. I just got back from a meeting in Ontario and I'm paying my folks a visit."

I cocked a brow at the mention of his parents, who were pretty awful people as far as I was concerned. "And how is *that* going?"

"About how you'd expect," he replied with a long and drawn-out sigh, and that actually did get a real laugh out of me, despite how hard my ribs were aching. Alton and I had always been on the same page with regard to his parents, and when he and I did talk, they were a frequent topic of conversation.

"Hey..." The tone of his voice picked up, excitement pushing through the words, "why, uh, why don't I pop by and take Sicily for a few days? Just so you can recover without having to worry too much about work?"

I opened my mouth to reply but clamped it shut when I felt my lower lip start to tremble. He just sounded so... hopeful and he hadn't spoken to Sicily in a few weeks, now, even though he had tried to call her on the regular. But Sicily wouldn't talk to him, not since the fog, and now, I was going to have to break his heart again. It wasn't that she didn't want to talk to him, but she had no way of explaining why she didn't want to see him—she couldn't tell him it was owing to her worry that all of us were contaminated. I figured in some instances, it was easier just to avoid the person in question. Not that I felt good about it, because I didn't.

"I'm sorry, Alton, but Sicily's not feeling good, either. She's got the same thing I do." I had to shut my eyes to keep my voice steady, taking even breaths so the sudden itch to cry would pass. I hadn't cried since I'd become a vampire and I didn't want to start now—besides, I wasn't sure if I even could cry or maybe I'd cry bloody tears? Yeah, not something I wanted to find out anytime soon.

"Oh."

"I, uh, I wouldn't want you to catch whatever we've got, so it's probably not a good idea to get together. Besides," I added quickly, glancing at the clock, "it's one o'clock on a Tuesday. She's still in school right now." Even though she wasn't.

I heard Alton exhale from the other end. "Yeah, I know," he said, and I bit my lip as I heard all the joy fade from his voice. "I just... well, I just sort of hoped she might give me a call later—when she gets home from school. I haven't heard from her in... a while."

"I know and... I'm... I'm sorry, Alton." I rubbed the bridge of my nose as I felt my headache travel down behind my eyeballs. God, I hated lying, especially to people like Alton. He'd done nothing but try and be the best father he could be and he was beyond fair with me. I could tell he hoped to be more —if not lovers, then friends, but he was just too far out of my loop for me to be able to talk to him openly and honestly.

"I miss her, Twila," he said softly.

I felt the sting of tears pricking my eyes. "I promise I'm not... I'm not keeping you from her or anything like that."

"I don't know what I did," he insisted. "It's like... one day she just turned her back on me and as far as I can tell, for no reason."

"It's nothing you did. She... she's just... well, she's just going through her... teenage years and everything is so up and down, you know?"

"I guess."

"Just give her time, Alton, and I know she'll come around. She's just... difficult right now." And on that account, I did feel like I was telling the truth.

Alton went silent. I could hear the crackle of the shotty network over the receiver and worried the call was going to disconnect, I sat up and cleared my throat. "Al?"

I hadn't called him by his nickname in years and I wasn't sure what prompted me to do so now. All the same, I heard the shifting of cloth, which told me that the line was still on. Alton let out a slow sigh that tugged at my tear ducts, and he sniffed, shuffling something as if readjusting the phone from hand to hand.

"Twila..." He whispered my name, and I could hear his throat tighten around the word—like it hurt him as much to say it as it hurt me to hear it. "What did I do wrong?"

My tears fell before I could even respond and they weren't blood tears. They looked to be the same as anyone else's. My chest caved into itself and I leaned over my lap, hand over the microphone so Alton couldn't hear me cry.

"She was such a happy little girl. Our little genius." His voice wasn't broken, but there was a certain instability to it as he continued. "I don't understand what happened. I thought I was doing everything right, being a good dad, but now she... she's freezing me out. And... well, I had no other choice than to contact you so I could find out... well, find out what I could have possibly done."

"Like I said, it wasn't anything you did."

He sighed. "I just... I have a hard time believing that... there must have been something." He sighed again. "Anyway, I hate having to go through you, Twila, and I'm sorry, I really am. But if you know what I said, or if it was something I did... please... please tell me. Whatever it is, I want to make it right with her."

We both went quiet this time, and the silence hung between us even longer. I wiped my tears away and breathed in deeply until they left my throat, but even as I started to respond, I knew nothing I could say would ease his pain. Being separated from your kid wasn't something that can be comforted with words. Especially when the true reason why can't be shared.

"You didn't do anything wrong, Alton," I said again quietly. "I know it's hard to believe, but you didn't, I promise. Sicily is... things are just stressful around here. She's dealing with it in her own way. We all are. She still talks about you, she still mentions visiting you, things are just... weird—she's very hormonal lately and everything is drama with her." I wiped my eyes again. "She's gonna come around eventually though, I promise. I don't want you to worry about that."

"How can I not worry about it?"

I nodded and thought to myself that it was long past time that Sicily saw her father. It had been a year since the fog had changed everything and I couldn't imagine we were still contagious. And if I were wrong? Well, then, we'd just welcome Alton into the fold. Which meant I'd have to see him all the time.

Yeah, that didn't exactly thrill me.

"I'll talk with her tonight and I'll tell her to give you a call back after dinner, okay?" I offered, hoping this small token would appease him—at least for the time being.

I knew the call would never come because for however guilty I felt about Alton, Sicily felt even guiltier which made her only want to avoid him all the more—while promising herself she'd solve this whole fog business in order to have a relationship with her father again. It wasn't much, but I had to give him something. I could almost feel the air lighten around him and he gave a small chuckle.

"Okay. Thanks, Twila. I appreciate it. I, uh... I hope you feel better soon."

"Thanks."

"Sure. I'll, uh, I'll talk to you later."

I listened to the hum of the disconnected call for a long time after he hung up. Then I let my cell phone fall from my hand and tipped sideways on the couch, grabbing a blanket from under the coffee table to wrap around myself. All the things that had happened within the last year... they weren't just affecting the three small towns the fog had spread through. The fog hadn't just changed people, it had taken those same people away from others. People like Alton, people like Sicily. I curled in tighter when I realized how helpless they must feel about it. Alton trying desperately to get into some kind of contact with his daughter. And Sicily... Sicily trying to help, trying to do what she felt was right. Trying to do anything she could to figure out how to make things better.

Maybe she was right. Maybe it wasn't River's Edge or Windy Ridge that was holding her back.

Maybe it was me.

All the feelings—the rottenness, the guilt, the worry and fear and stress of it all—wrapped around me just like the blanket, and all those feelings cradled me, arms tight and firm as I drifted off to sleep.

Chapter Eleven

The sky was darkening when I opened my eyes.

In the first few moments after doing so, the trailer seemed calm, with the exception of the scraping sound of the wind blowing branches against the windows. My head had stopped aching, and I figured my body must have recovered from the sunlight-sickness, though I still felt a twinge in my muscles when I pushed myself up into a sitting position.

None of the lights were on, but my night vision kicked in and as I blinked the sleep from my eyes, I saw a mug full of fresh blood sitting on the coffee table with a note resting beside it. On the note were two pale pills I recognized as nausea medication likely taken from Ol' Ned's stash. I rolled my eyes, but grabbed them anyway, tossing the pills into my mouth before draining the cup. I didn't think the medication was going to do anything, really, but I appreciated the thought. There was no way Ol' Ned would have been brave enough to come back inside after the fuss I'd made, so I assumed the present was a peace offering from Sicily, a suspicion that was proved the minute I picked up the note.

Sorry about skipping class again. I won't do it again, I promise. I understand you were worried. I'm sorry I didn't take that into account. I called Dad back while you were asleep and he was really happy to hear from me. If I can prove the fog isn't contagious, and we will know that soon—if Sheriff Dean or Mason change into anything—I think I'll visit Dad in a few months. Just so you know.

Hope you feel better soon.

I folded the note between my fingers. It *did* make me feel a bit better to know that Sicily had taken the initiative with Alton. My guess was that she'd been eavesdropping on our conversation, and she'd gotten a good old-fashioned accidental guilt trip. I smirked a little and stood, stretching out my sore back. Nice to know that children eavesdropping could work in my favor, for once.

As soon as I stood up, there was a dull *thud* that came from the kitchen, and when I stepped toward it, I saw Sicily at the dining table, the surface of it completely covered in binders. One of them was open in front of her, and considering the Elmer's Glue Stick sitting beside her, she appeared to be pasting something inside it, scrapbook-style.

One of Sicily's goals over the past few months was to take a census of everyone in Damnation

County so policing ourselves would become easier. Her binder was full of names and addresses of residents, pictures, and short biographies from folk all around us, or at least as many as she could find. Turns out, turning into a monstrosity over the course of a day had made some folk distrusting. Furthermore, not everyone was excited to give her the information she was looking for—I guess turning into rodents and the like isn't exactly information people want out there, circulating. And that was another good point—were Sicily's information to fall into the wrong hands, it could be devastating. That was why I'd made her promise to keep her log locked in a lockbox out in the storage shed behind the trailer—a place I didn't imagine anyone would ever find it.

Now, I slowly approached her, head ducked with a sheepish look. "Hi," I said, and she glanced up with a blink, offering me a shy smile in return. "Thanks for the mug. I know you hate dealing with that stuff."

Sicily shrugged and smoothed out her paste work. "You weren't feeling well. It's no biggie." She ran her fingers along the edges of the paper and I frowned, walking beside her to peer down at her work. To my surprise, she was pasting what appeared to be a photocopied version of the shifter sketch Mason Hawke had completed.

"Hey!" I tapped it with a finger. "Where'd you get this?"

Sicily turned to me with a rather mischievous-looking grin. "Sheriff Hawke."

I started. *"What?"*

"Don't worry, Mama, I didn't steal it... jeez," she laughed.

"I didn't think you had. I just... how in the world did you end up with it?"

She shrugged. "Sheriff Hawke came by while you were asleep and he gave it to me. He said he was going door-to-door to try and see if anyone's seen the guy on the poster and he said I was the first one who actually answered when he knocked." She looked me up and down. "And he said he wanted to check up on you. Make sure you're doing okay."

My neck started to burn at the thought that Dean had come by while I'd been asleep—luckily it wasn't as though I slept upside down or with my eyes open so hopefully he hadn't noticed anything off about me. Regardless, I scoffed and tried to play my reaction off as a dismissal, but really, hearing that Dean had asked after me made my stomach flutter. Sicily kept smiling.

"Y'know, he's pretty darn hot." She smoothed down the pasted sketch casually, though I could see her glancing at me from the corner of her eye. "And really considerate, seems like."

"Oh, quit it." I gave her a playful shove.

"What? You don't think he's hot?"

I looked at her and frowned. "Dean is... well, he's Dean."

"What's that mean?"

"Nothing," I answered, starting to sound exasperated.

"I don't think he thinks of you as 'Twila being Twila'," she continued with a big smile.

"What's that mean?" I mimicked her and then stuck my tongue out when she gave me a look.

"It means... he came by to see if you were okay and he seems to be checking up on you a lot."

"This is a small town and I'm one of the few people he was... accustomed to."

"I'm just saying... seems to me that the sheriff might still be burnin' a candle for you, Mama."

I laughed. And then wasn't sure what to make of the heat that crept across my cheeks. "The sheriff," I started and then corrected myself. "*Dean* is just being the kind, considerate person he is. And as far as he and I go, there is no candle. It burned out a long time ago."

"Hmm, doesn't seem that way to me."

"Well, that's how it is."

"I don't think Sheriff Dean thinks that's how it is."

I looked at her. "Sicily, I swear you could make a tree lose its temper."

"I'm just saying," she started with a laugh and an innocent expression.

"And I'm just saying Dean and I were high school sweethearts, that's it."

"High school sweethearts who nearly ran away together," I heard her mumble, but she thankfully dropped the subject as we both studied the sketch together. Then she looked up at me. "Clearly, you didn't give Mason the full picture."

"Clearly," I answered with a clipped nod.

She looked back at the drawing. "What did you leave out?"

"Pink skin, bristles all over his body, and tusks from his underslung jaw."

Her eyebrows reached for the ceiling. "You left out a lot."

"Yep."

She nodded. "So, what kind of a shifter do you think it was?"

"Some kind of hog-man, if I had to guess." I walked to the fridge and found some fresh blood to pour into my mug. "It's probably one of the crazies that ran off when the fog came and the poor man just never regained his senses. He was hungry, too. Ate the diner outta house and home."

"A hog-shifter. That's a new one." Sicily stood with her binder and pulled a corkboard out from behind one of our cabinets. On it were photos of all the missing people we'd been trying to track down since the fog came in. Among the other things Sicily had done for the town, keeping track of those who still needed to be found was the most invaluable. She'd even noted which missing people we'd located but hadn't managed to capture yet, their last known locations scribbled beneath their photos on spare strips of paper. As to what we'd do with the creatures we eventually captured but couldn't reintroduce to proper society? We hadn't quite worked out a solution though the word 'zoo' had been thrown around plenty. I still wasn't sure how I felt about that.

We stood side-by-side, comparing every picture on her board to the sketch, though my eyes instantly went to one in particular. In the center of the corkboard was the largest of the pictures, a posed photograph of four men standing beside a freshly caught deer. Nowadays, it was strange to see what Bud, Ol' Ned, and Boone used to look like; Bud was still just as heavy as before, but when he was human, he'd had the biggest grin, and a patchy black beard surrounding it that blended into his hair. Ol' Ned was thinner than his lizard-man counterpart and his smile was more patchwork, his fingers and face smeared with oil from his tinkering, and Boone had slick black hair and thick brows across his face. Now he was as hairless as a dolphin.

But highlighting the monster hunters before they became monsters, themselves, wasn't the reason the photo was pinned to the middle of the board. That honor was given to the man who was standing in between Bud and Ol' Ned. The man was in his sixties when the photo was taken. A rail-thin gentleman, he had a long, white beard, sported a bulbous nose and worn-down overalls alongside a warm expression. 'Slim Jim' was the name we'd given him —purely because 'Jimmy-Joe-Jay-Bob' was a mouthful and then some. Regardless, Slim Jim had disappeared shortly after the fog arrived. He'd been Bud, Ol' Ned, and Boone's friend for over fifty years before he'd vanished, and, if I was being honest, he was also the reason the monster-hunting group was formed in the first place. The boys had been looking for Slim Jim for months, insisting that he was still alive. Even though I'd liked Slim Jim just as much as the next person, I wasn't as sure about his survival, but I didn't want to crush their spirits. Bud seemed to hold on to the most hope for Slim Jim's survival and kept this same picture in his pocket at all times.

The shifter in Mason's drawing had too broad a face to be Slim Jim, and as far as I could see, the man in the drawing didn't match any of the other missing people on her board, either.

"Doesn't look familiar," I said. "I kind of figured he'd be from out of town, anyway. Maybe Dagwood or Devil's Run." Well, if what Dorcas had yelled was right.

"Well, that doesn't mean a whole lot these days." Sicily tapped the photo of Bud and Ol' Ned. "Neither one of them look like they used to, either. For all we know, this hog-shifter could be an old drifter and we'd never know. If we can track him down, though, maybe we'll be able to watch him unshift and figure out who it is."

"If he can unshift."

My stomach curled. Just thinking about Sicily "tracking him down" made me nervous, because she seemed to conveniently forget she was still human and as such, fragile. I turned to her gently and put my hand on hers, slowly guiding it until the binder was pressed shut.

"... Sicily, can you take a break for a while? For me?" I asked, giving her a sincere expression of concern. Sicily looked up at me and I saw her face soften at my tired expression. "Just... I need some peace. We can go back to the monster details later, but just for now, just until Dean and Mason leave town, could we maybe press pause for the sake of my sanity?"

She frowned. "What makes you think they're going to leave town?"

I breathed in deeply because it was the same question I'd repeatedly asked myself. "I don't know."

"I don't think they're leaving town any time soon, Mama. It looked to me like Sheriff Hawke was pretty much here to stay."

"That's what I'm worried about."

Sicily paused. For a flickering moment, it looked like she was going to concede and give me a night's peace, but she pinched her lip between her teeth in an oddly nervous way. Then she looked at me, eyes shining with guilt, and instantly I felt the hairs on the back of my neck stand at attention.

"Sicily." I stepped back a bit to look at her fully. "What's that look for?"

Her eyes flicked away from me. "I... don't think we can break from the monster hunting just yet."

I swallowed down a lump in my throat. "And why is that?"

"Well, when the guys were here earlier," she started, fiddling with the sleeve of her shirt, "we may have been discussing the shifter."

"The hog-man?"

She nodded. "The hog-man."

"And?"

"And we may have... heard rumors of something hooved staggering through the woods." Her head was fully hung low now, like a dog's tail tucked between its legs. "And... they may be out setting a trap for it."

"They're setting a trap for it?" I repeated, feeling my nerves starting to fray all over again. Sicily nodded. "When?"

"Like. Right now."

I stared at her and she shrunk further in on herself. Then I let out a quiet, vicious curse and immediately set the mug back onto the counter, turning on my heel and racing back to my bedroom. I didn't have enough time to get my proper hunting clothes out, but I had to get out of my work clothes, so I threw on some pants and sneakers and skidded my way back to the front door.

"Sicily," I turned to face her before I left the trailer. And when I looked at her, I *really* looked at her. "Stay. *Put.*"

She nodded, and, with a sigh, I dashed into the darkness of the evening, trying to prep myself to deal with whatever idiocy the boys were in the process of cooking up.

Chapter Twelve

Stressed out as I was, the only thing that seemed to help was running at night.

Sicily appeared to have allowed me to sleep in after our argument, because usually I'd be up at sundown, ready to head into the diner for my shift. No doubt Sicily figured Dorcas wouldn't need me for a few days considering she had to basically restock the entire kitchen.

Instead, I got to enjoy the sweetness of pure nighttime air. Similar to the way in which sunlight made me sick, nighttime invigorated me. What little aches, lethargy, or nausea that caught me during the day disappeared the moment the sun set—it was like my youth returned to me with the embrace of the darkness, the shadows. I'd never been a very fit person in my human life, but this supernatural shift had given my body a boost in both speed and strength, but also in vitality. I felt strangely more alive in this form than I ever had before—usually right after I fed.

River's Edge Trailer Park was quiet that evening. The dirt roads were empty, though I could see lights from the surrounding trailers. I couldn't help but grieve for the folks who were stuck inside because of the normies (aka Mason and Dean) in Windy Ridge. Nocturnal beings had it the roughest, considering most of living time seemed to go on during the day—now they couldn't even enjoy the night for fear of running into the sheriff.

Regardless, it was nice having the area to myself as I sprinted full speed towards the forest's edge. I'd tied my hair in a ponytail and dressed in stretch pants and a running bra, wanting nothing more than to feel the wind against my cheeks. And now, as I felt exactly that, I focused on the steady movement of my muscles as my feet hit the dirt. It felt like I was running more on a cloud than on soil. I moved so fast, it didn't actually feel like my feet were falling onto the ground, but more that the ground was rushing beneath me.

For as great as it felt to be one of the wild things in the night, I had a problem—I didn't know *where* in the forest the boys had gone. And the woods were a massive thing, stretching miles from the mountains. The first stop, I decided, would be Bud's trailer, just to see if I could find any clues as to where the boys had gone. Seeing as how Bud was the unannounced head of the investigative team, it made sense to me that the boys would have met up at his trailer.

Bud was the only one on the monster team who didn't live in River's Edge Trailer Park. Instead, he lived in a double-wide in the middle of the forest because he 'valued his privacy something fierce'.

It didn't take me more than five minutes to run there, and I gulped in lungfuls of the night air as I pushed the door open and took a peek inside. As expected, the place was a mess, with papers and scraps of metal from Bud's traps littering the floor. All along one wall were boxes that were piled so high, they made up their own wall. Just like Ol' Ned, Bud was a hoarder and then some and proof was in all the crap that littered his trailer—filling it up to such an extent that you had to wade your way through all the junk.

After managing to do just that, I found my way to his kitchen table which had been moved to the middle of the floor (probably because the walls of trash were threatening to come down on top of it). When I walked over, sure enough, I spotted a map which had been drawn on a wide sheet of paper. There was one of Ol' Ned's diagram beside the map, detailing what looked to be a tripwire-net trap, but the map itself revealed a red circle in an area about a mile from the forest's entrance.

"You idiots better still be there," I mumbled to myself as I breathed in a big breath and shook my head. "And the three of you better be okay."

I double-checked the map, nodded to myself,

and then started back through the alley of crap that led to the front door. After closing the door behind me and walking down the rickety old porch steps, once again I was off, sprinting lightning-fast through the seemingly neverending trees.

From the looks of the map, the boys had gone to the patch of forest that was near the slope to Windy Hill, right at the edge of the residential area of Windy Ridge. It was now a *little* more understandable as to why they'd decided to rush off without me, considering the sheriff's office was right up the hill. Well, not only that, but I was pretty sure the three of them were afraid of me after my outburst and probably were giving me time to calm down.

Regardless, I flew through the trees and the last outcropping of houses until I reached a dirt road that led up to Windy Hill, all the while keeping my eyes peeled for any sign of my boys, which, ironically, made me miss the shadowed figure that rounded a corner just as I approached it.

The two of us locked eyes for a split second, just as I managed to avert my course before I would have smacked right into him (and I was fairly sure it was a 'him' given how dang tall he was). Digging my heels into the dirt so I could skid to a halt, I then found myself panting as I fought to catch my breath and whipped around, suddenly staring right into Dean Hawke's eyes.

I stopped dead.

He was dressed casually, not in his sheriff's uniform, and had a leather satchel around his neck, looking like he was going bird-watching or the like.

He looked at me in surprise, glancing up to peer at the half-formed moon above.

"Twila." His eyes flicked up and down my figure. "What are you doing out here at this time of night?"

I wanted to ask him the same question, but it was obvious what he was doing—his job. Even if he wasn't dressed like it. Instantly, I felt my nerves go on edge, but I still offered him a (closed-lipped) smile in response. "Oh, just wanted to get out for a walk."

"At the far end of town, on your way up to Windy Hill which is... *far* from River's Edge."

I nodded. "Well, when you put it like that—"

"It sounds weird."

I gave this strange, choked sort of laugh that more sounded like I was having a stroke. "Weird. Yeah. Ha." He looked at me and one eyebrow arched up suspiciously. "This is, uh, well, it's the only time I get to myself, really."

Dean raised the other eyebrow. "Do I need to remind you we've got a dangerous criminal on the loose?" He didn't wait for me to respond. "Apparently, I do."

"Ha, well," I smoothed back the stray bits of my hair as I fought for some reasonable explanation as to what I was doing in the middle of nowhere in the middle of the night. And... nothing came. "Right, sort of forgot about that." He gave me that distrusting expression of his again. "But good point and noted." Then I tapped my head, as if to say his point had been recorded in my brain. "And don't you worry about me."

"That's exactly what I'm doing."

I smiled again, touched even as I was still uncomfortable. "Well, don't. I can, uh, I can take care of myself."

Dean didn't look reassured, and I didn't blame him. His sudden appearance had surprised me, and I could feel my voice shaking, so to distract him I gestured to him with a quick wave, shifting my weight with my hand on my hip. "What about you? You on duty?"

"I am." He opened the flap of the satchel and pulled out a stack of papers that I quickly recognized as the shifter's sketch. "I'm handing these out to see if anyone recognizes the man. Trying to get word out wherever I can."

I motioned to his street clothes. "You aren't in uniform?"

He glanced down at himself and gave me a sheepish smile. "Only so long a uniform can go without being washed." Then he chuckled. "I'm embarrassed to say I'm not much good at keeping on top of my laundry. And neither is Mason."

"Men," I answered with a laugh as I shook my head and strangely felt like I wanted to offer to do his laundry for him. It was a weird thought because I didn't consider myself especially domestically motivated. Sicily was better about doing the dishes and the laundry than I was.

"Men," he repeated and then gave me that

devil's smile which made my heartbeat increase. Good Lord, but Dean Hawke was one darned good-looking man.

"How's, uh, how's that going?"

"How's what going?"

"Handing out flyers?"

Dean wilted a bit. "No one seems to be interested in opening their doors." And then I remembered how Sicily had said Dean had stopped by earlier. He must have been making his rounds ever since. Talk about dedication.

"Sicily said you, uh, stopped by."

He nodded, closing the distance between us as he put a hand on my shoulder. "Yeah, I wanted to see how you were doing." Then his gaze dropped, and he took me in from head to toe and I felt my heart start pounding in earnest. There was just something in his eyes—something that said he liked what he saw.

"I'm," I started at the same time that he said, "You seem to be doing much better."

"Yeah," I said with that strange laugh again. "I'm fine."

He nodded and just continued staring at me while his eyes seemed to burn in their chocolate depths. And though I didn't want to admit it, I very much enjoyed the way his eyes slowly rolled down over my neck, to my breasts and then down to my hips. I was still painfully aware of his hand on my shoulder and the way he trailed it down the length of my arm, as if he knew he should step away but was fighting it. I flashed him another smile and reached out, placing my hand on top of his and I squeezed it slightly as a mark of thanks. "I'm alright, I promise. Nothing but a few sore muscles."

Dean brought his attention from my hand to my face and grinned at me, his teeth white in the moonlight. "I'm glad to hear it. Though that's part of the reason why I was surprised to see you out here. You took a fair beating earlier."

That last comment gave me some pause. "Yeah, I'm okay."

"I'd say you're more than okay."

And I couldn't speak for a moment. My heart was in my throat, prohibiting any words from leaving my lips. And Dean didn't say anything either. We both just stood there, me staring up at him and him staring down at me. He took a step closer and I didn't know what to do. I didn't know what *he* was going to do—say something else? Kiss me? Hug me?

It may have been the shadows across his face, but I swore I saw a bit of red curl into Dean's cheeks as he cleared his throat. "Well," he met my eyes once more. "What I meant to say was... you are the same Twila I knew all those years ago and..."

He didn't finish his sentence, just lifted his hand and reached out with his index finger to gently trace the line of my cheek, from below my eye, down to the start of my hairline above my ear. Then he tucked what must have been a stray tendril of hair behind my ear and the breath caught in my throat.

"And?" I whispered.

He chuckled, and the sound was rich. Throaty and deep. Sexy. Good Lord but the man was like sex incarnate. "And I have to admit... you've been on my mind." He grew quiet then and I could suddenly hear the increase in his heart rate. It was as if someone had put a stethoscope to my ears and his heart because his heart was beating so loud, it was as if it were echoing against the trunks of the trees.

It took a second before I felt the blush set in. My entire face felt like it was on fire, and I couldn't even hide it because we were standing so close together. The only thing I could think to do was laugh and push him (probably too hard) in the chest so I could have enough space to breathe and, hopefully, to think. It was just—with Dean standing this close—thinking was a tough thing to do.

"Well, *thank* you for your concern, Sheriff, but—"

And then he kissed me.

Just like that.

I was in the middle of saying something completely stupid and the words were taken right out of my mouth when I felt Dean's arms loop around my shoulders, pulling me into the heat of his chest, and then his mouth was on mine and mine was on his. And he kissed me with tongue—just like he'd kissed me when we were teenagers and my body responded the same way—with a yearning I'd never known since Dean had walked out of my life. Well, I knew it again—I knew it now, and I knew it with a fever that I hadn't felt in way too long.

And then I remembered who I was. *What* I was. And I remembered who Dean was and a cold sweat washed over me, killing the mood instantly. I broke away from his embrace and took a step back.

"I, uh, I should probably get back," I managed.

He breathed in deeply and there was regret in his eyes. "I'm... I'm sorry I did that. I told myself I wasn't going to."

"Don't apologize," I managed, when all I really wanted to say was 'do it again'. But he couldn't do it again and I couldn't allow him to do it again, because this couldn't happen. Whatever *this* was, if it was even anything, it was bad. Really, really bad.

"I forgot myself," he continued, frowning down at me. "It just felt like—"

"Old times?"

He nodded then paused. "Old times, yes, but new times too."

I smiled up at him and had to fight the urge to step on my tip-toes to kiss him again. But kissing Dean was an absolute no. Especially when he was dangerously close to the area where the boys were investigating. And the last thing I wanted Dean to stumble across was any evidence of the truth as to what was really going on in Windy Ridge. And that was when I got an idea.

"Would you, um, would you walk me home?"

He seemed a bit surprised, no doubt thinking back to the time when I'd said I could take care of myself, but he didn't let his surprise faze him and, instead, nodded immediately. "Of course. I'd be happy to."

To Dean it might have been a romantic suggestion, but I was more interested in leading him away from whatever the boys were up to. And once he walked me home, and I said goodnight to him, I could make my way to the forest again and put the fear of God into the three impulsive hillbillies.

"Twila?" he started and when I looked up into those deep brown eyes, I got scared. Scared he was going to say something I didn't know how to respond to—scared he was going to put a voice to the feelings that were obviously running through the both of us.

"Race you back?" The words just flew out of my lips and before I knew it, I'd already taken a couple of leaps away from him.

He looked shell-shocked for a moment, not that I could blame him, but then there seemed to be an excitement in his expression as he faced me with that boyish grin that took me back twenty-three years.

"What do I get if I win?"

I laughed. "What makes you so sure you'll win?"

He shrugged. "I'm fast. Always have been."

Well, there was no way he was as fast as me, but I kept that little tidbit to myself. "What do you want if you win?"

Dean laughed and thought for a moment, before glancing back at me again. "How about... I get to take you to dinner?"

I blinked at him, surprised. He... he *was* flirting with me, wasn't he? Good Lord, I had far too much to worry about without adding *this—whatever this was—*to the list. Yet, my heart didn't quite agree. Instead, it about lifted into my head. I bit back a fresh smile and folded my arms as I tried to remind myself that anything between Dean and me needed to be nipped in the bud before it ever even had the chance to germinate.

"You're on."

He winked as he caught up to me, making a motion of setting up his position to start the run.

I found myself getting excited for an entirely different reason. "Well," I said, keeping my voice steady, despite my nerves. "I hope your pride doesn't get hurt easily."

He opened his mouth to reply, his eyes glinting with a challenge, but I took off without another word.

Chapter Thirteen

It was surprisingly hard to keep my pace slow.

In my new vampire state, I'd never raced a human before—the only time I'd really tested my speed was against other monsters and only for Sicily's experiments. We'd never found anyone who could beat me, at least not out of the current residents of Windy Ridge. True, there were things in the woods we hadn't found yet, and I stayed humble when I remembered that sooner or later, I was gonna find something to beat me. Dean, however, was not that thing.

It almost felt like more of a workout *not* to go at full speed. If I wasn't paying full attention (if I looked behind myself to respond to a taunt or see him smile), I would feel myself speed up significantly and then I'd have to actively tense my calves and slow my pace. Dean was putting up the best fight he could, but he really had no chance. Racing Dean now reminded me of a time when Sicily was just a kid and wanted to race me to the playground. I still remembered her laughter when I'd let her win every time. But Dean *wasn't* my daughter, and I wasn't going to give him the same grace.

"How's the weather back there?" I called behind me as we ran through the business district sidewalks (most of which were closed and boarded up). We'd been going hard for a few minutes, but Dean wasn't as winded as I expected him to be, and he smirked as I turned my head to glance back at him.

"Not bad! Can't wait for you to experience it, too!"

I laughed and shook my head. "Not on your life, Sheriff! Enjoy the view back there."

I heard Dean laugh and it took me a second to realize my accidental innuendo, and embarrassment flooded me instantly. Part of me wanted to turn around, to correct myself—to tell him I hadn't meant anything untoward by it, but I decided to let it pass for the sake of the race.

A good part of me *did* want to fall behind, though, so I could have a view of my own.

We reached the diner and wrapped around it, heading into what was passed as the 'fancy' part of town—as in there used to be two stores in this section that hadn't sold general items at clearance prices. Both of them were closed now though.

Just for fun, I slowed enough to let Dean reach my side and caught him grinning at me.

"You're—" (pant-pant) "A lot faster than I remember," he said as he looked me over. "You musta taken up running as a hobby?"

I gave a nervous sort of laugh and shrugged, adding artificial breaths to my voice to sound like I, too, was panting, but the truth was this was more like a nice, jaunt around town for me. "Um." Taken up running? That was a good excuse. "Sort of, yeah. The insomnia's hit pretty hard over the last year."

"Well, hey, props for choosing a healthy alternative." He started to edge past me, but I overtook him once again, sticking closer to his side in order to hear him as he spoke. "Most folk go for the drink when that happens."

"Drinks don't affect me anymore." The words slipped out of my mouth before I realized what I'd said and in realizing it, started to panic. Dean, meanwhile, gave me a raised-eyebrows look as my throat tightened.

"Why d'you say that?"

"Oh, I just mean… I have a high tolerance." I started to speed up again, cursing my stupid tongue underneath my breath. I was getting too relaxed around him, too relaxed when talking to him. He was frustratingly nice to spend time with, like he hadn't changed from the loveable young man he used to be. I had to remind myself that I'd had a goal in mind when I started this silly race—that being to ditch him—so I kicked up my pace and left him in the dust as I led him around the buildings.

We were approaching the end of the neighborhood area of Windy Ridge, with the Dooley manor rising over the grounds before us. My plan was to turn, cut across the street at the border of the forest and then lead us back to the lower-income homes and eventually, River's Edge and my trailer. All told, that was at least two miles, and by that point, I hoped Dean would be too tired and he'd let me go on home by myself (at which point, I'd turn around and immediately head after those sorry hillbillies I called friends).

I was a good few feet ahead of Dean when we began to approach the Dooley's front lawn, so I was able to see Karen Dooley in all her red-deviled glory. And I was fairly sure Dean would see her too —as soon as he caught up to me. As I faced her and the blood started to drain out of my head, I took in her pinched and furious face which grew even redder with anger once she recognized me. Then she began marching her way toward me from her front door. My heartrate started to pound something fierce and I felt my face twist in horror as I searched for something to say or do. One thing I did know? I had to act quickly; all it took was Dean to get one good look at Karen and our entire cover was blown. That, or she'd get shot, and I was too good of a person to *really* hope for that to happen.

At least, I thought I was too good a person.

There was only one way to go—one thing to do. While there was a path around the Dooley manner, a patch of dense forest separated the well-to-dos from the poor people, and without much thought, I glanced back to Dean, making sure he was looking at me as I cut across the street and dashed into the woods.

I kept an eye out behind me just to make sure he was following, and sure enough, I could hear the panting. I should've anticipated seeing Karen again, but to be honest, all my focus was on Dean and praying he wouldn't notice the fuming devil-woman standing in front of her house. And if he did notice her, it was my hope that he'd think she was just a Halloween prop—which was a silly thought considering it was nowhere near Halloween.

Regardless, the issue known as Karen Dooley was something I'd have to tackle later. Generally, when I pissed Karen off in one way or another (which was a usual occurrence), my failsafe was to send Sicily over to talk Karen down. Most the time Sicily threatened to cut Karen off from getting new clothes made (I'd become the go-to seamstress of Windy Ridge since I was the best with needle and thread), and that almost always got Karen to put that pointy tail of hers back between her legs, where it belonged. She'd always lived a life of semi-luxury, even for someone in the middle of nowhere, and she hadn't learned to sew so much as a button on a coat, let alone a whole outfit. I was the only one in town who was talented enough to sew clothing for monsters, so usually, Karen backed down pretty fast. Now, though, I wasn't sure if that threat would still work. Karen looked mighty irritated.

As to me—my endurance was still going strong

and I continued to run my feet into the pavement, barely feeling any burn in my muscles. If I pushed myself, I could run for thirty to forty-five minutes at top speed without stopping, so this simple run was a breeze, even with the uneven terrain. I still kept an ear out for Dean, though, in case he decided to give up and wave his white flag of surrender. He may have been panting, now, his strides getting somewhat shorter the longer we went on, but it still surprised me how long he was lasting. Which obviously meant I had to somehow slow him down—that is if I ever wanted to get out to the woods where Boone and the rest of the boys were, no doubt, getting themselves into trouble.

"Need a break?" I shouted as I turned around to face him, slowing ever so slightly so he could better hear my voice. Dean gave a raspy scoff in reply, though I couldn't see his expression thanks to darkness around us.

"Why? Do *you* need one, Twila?" I heart him reply and couldn't help my smile. If only he knew the half of it... "That make-believe first place trophy getting too heavy in your hands?"

"Ha! No, sir." I grinned to myself. "I'm fit as a fiddle, thank you very much."

"Yeah," Dean laughed. "I can see as much."

We kept going. I kept dodging between the trees and leaping over logs, doing everything I could to tire the man out. Yet, he was almost keeping pace with me, and I was beginning to worry that my attempt to get him to surrender wasn't going to go as planned. He seemed to be gaining on me, in fact, as

I heard footsteps growing louder as they trampled the forest debris. I glanced behind and catching the whites of his eyes in the sliver of moonlight that bled through the canopy overhead, realized Dean was still far away, and still scrambling to keep up. Instead, the noises I was hearing seemed to be coming from in front of me, now that I thought about it. I didn't realize what they were until it was too late.

A flash of pink streaked across my vision.

That was followed by a sharp squeal, both human and pig-like, echoing endlessly into the air. Something hit me from my side, and I didn't even have time to scream before I was hauled ass-over-teakettle into the air. I could just barely see the whiskered face of what I was fairly sure was the hog-man before it crashed into me, throwing me backwards through the air. I felt my skull crack on a nearby tree, which dazed me and hurt like a 'summa bitch' as Bud would say.

It was maybe a second later that I realized the hit to my head was worse than I'd thought because my world started to spin, stars streaking past one another as though they were circling me in a twister. Another second after that, I collapsed, blackness overcoming me as I fought to keep consciousness.

I could hear shouts in the distance, one voice was Dean's, but there were three others I didn't recognize. That is until I forced myself to sit upright, blinked the stars out of my vision, and saw the figures approaching. My vision doubled, but I still managed to see three monstrous men hollering like idiots as they chased the pink, bristled shifter further into the woods. My head throbbed, but I was still steady enough to feel the rage bubbling in my gut. Of course, Ol' Ned, Bud, and Boone would have run the danged shifter right into me, giving me a concussion to boot.

As soon as my eyes uncrossed, I was prepared to kick each and every *one* of their hillbilly butts all the way to Arkansas. But I was spared the chance as a set of footsteps approached me, though this time they were gentler. I groaned and rubbed my head, glancing up to see Dean's tall and broad figure standing over me. Only, he wasn't looking at me. His eyes were trained in the direction where my partners had run off to, and his face, previously flushed with exertion, was slowly turning a pale, ashy white.

"...Twila," he panted, pointing in their direction. "Did—did I just see what I think I saw?"

Apparently, he hadn't seen the thing bash me into the tree, because if he had, I would've hoped he'd more concerned for my well-being than the hog-man who'd disappeared into the woods. No point in alerting him to an injury which probably should have killed me.

Instead, I pushed to my feet and faced him with genuine interest as I tried to will the pounding in my head to recede. And it was doing just that—my hyper healing ability already in overdrive.

"What—what did you think you saw?" I mumbled. Secretly, my heart had started to pound as I wondered how in the heck I was gonna explain this one away. The rhythm of my now frantic heartbeat was sending shockwaves to the pain in the back of my head. I looked up at Dean and saw him floundering, the usual reaction of logic meeting the impossibility of reality.

"It was—it was...well, I don't know how to say this but..." And his voice faded away.

"Just spit it out."

He looked at me and his eyes were wide. Disbelieving. "I know it's going to sound as if I've lost my mind, Twila, but I believe I just saw a lizard, but it was *huge* and standing on two feet."

"That does sound like you've lost your mind," I managed.

But Dean wasn't even listening to me. He was still lost to his own shock and shaking his head. "And beside it—no... it just... it can't be," he said, still shaking his head although I could tell he was having an internal argument with himself—his eyes reporting one thing but his brain insisting it wasn't possible. "It couldn't have been the light... I know... I saw its face."

"You saw what's face? An animal?" I tried to lead him with the question but I was fairly sure he wouldn't be led away from what he'd seen. I knew, because I'd seen the same thing too—on many more occasions than Dean had.

He turned to me then and pointed at the footprint barely visible in the mud just beside me. The print was canine, sharp claws at the end of the toes, and far larger than any wolf's print ought to be.

"It looked like a... well, like a... a *wolf* man." Dean's gaze was steady, certain, as he laid it on me. "It was a man who looked like a wolf."

I bit my lip. My stomach churned, and I closed my eyes.

"Summa bitch."

Chapter Fourteen

I made sure Sicily went to bed before I got out the moonshine.

Prior to that, though, she was shocked when I lead Dean through the door of our trailer. And I could see the fear on her face when I gave her a whispered recap of the forest encounter with the shifter (of course, I only said as much as I walked her to her room, making sure we both were out of Dean's earshot).

"It nearly killed you again, Mama," she said beneath her breath, turning her big brown eyes on me.

I did my best to comfort her, told her that no matter what happened, everything was going to be okay, but to tell the truth, I was petrified. The boys were still out there and this hog-man was obviously dangerous. They needed me but I couldn't get to them until I got rid of Dean. For now, my thoughts were focused solely on getting him drunk on moonshine but that would take time I didn't have. Sicily was too smart for me to be able to lie to her anymore, as well. From the hug she gave me, I could tell she knew exactly how I felt.

Dean sat on the couch and I slowly poured the two of us a sizable portion, letting the water-clear liquid splash into two empty Mason jars, as was tradition. Moonshine didn't do anything for me anymore, but it wasn't right to drink it out of anything else.

We clinked glasses and drank, and Dean came up from his glass with a sharp whistle, his face screwing up humorously in surprise.

"Wow." He coughed and pressed his mouth to his sleeve as he shook his head. "Dorcas doesn't slow down. I forgot how strong this stuff is."

"That's because the last time you had it, you were just under the legal age," I replied with a smirk.

Dean laughed and raised his brows as he nodded, but I could tell his mind was elsewhere—on what he'd seen in the forest, for example. "I think I'm losing my mind."

"You're not losing your mind, Dean," I managed and then took in a deep breath as I purposely tried to find another subject of discourse. "You remember the last time we drank this stuff?" He looked at me in question. "We got busted with open containers by the old sheriff. I was underage, too, and I remember the absolute hell my pa gave me when they released us from the detention center."

"Right." Dean sighed and sat back into the couch, swishing the drink in his hand. "My grandpa wouldn't let me see you for a month afterward."

I nodded. "Yeah, that's right."

"It was one of the times he nearly made me break it off with you," he continued, pulling his gaze from the libation in his Mason jar and facing me, instead. "He thought you were a bad influence."

"*Me?* You're the one who introduced me to everything I wasn't supposed to know at that age," I laughed and he did too.

Then he shook his head and seemed lost in the past for a minute—a minute I was grateful for because it was one in which he wasn't thinking about the fact that he'd seen Ol' Ned and Bud in the forest earlier.

"So, I did." He gave a sad smile and stared out of the window then, smoothing his sleek black hair back behind his ears. It was even longer now, since the first day I'd seen him when he'd walked into the diner and back into my life. Of course, it made sense that it was longer because the barber in town was now some sort of marsupial.

"Is it weird that I kind of miss those days?" Dean asked as he looked up at me.

"The days when you had to break up with me?" I stuck out my tongue at him. He looked at me, surprised, and I quickly shook my head. "I'm kidding. No, it's not weird. Time sure does pass quick these days though."

"Yeah," he sighed as he looked around the sparse trailer, as if seeing beyond its walls. "I miss driving around these mountains and being out in the fresh Ozark air."

"Well, here you are." I clapped my hands together and motioned for him to take another swallow of the moonshine with me, to which he happily complied.

"Here I am."

"And yet you don't sound happy about that?"

He nodded. "I'm happy to serve the law, but I can't deny that I enjoyed the delinquency of my younger days. I think it was just the fun of being a teenager, running from the cops and your folks at the same time." He glanced at me with a wistful smile. "So... what happened to the old sheriff?"

I frowned at him. "You know what happened to him."

He nodded and got that knowing smile of his that did funny things to my insides. "Right. What *really* happened to him?"

I stilled for a moment. My eyes glazed a bit and I watched the low light reflect off the alcohol, nothing but the silence of the night around us.

"Well, he's dead." I gave a soft shrug.

"But what killed him?"

"Reports said it was an animal attack?"

"That's what the reports said," Dean continued with a brisk nod. "But I want to know what the truth is."

I frowned at him. "It sounds like you're implying—".

"I'm not implying anything," he interrupted while taking another sip of his moonshine. When he put the Mason jar down, I could see it was empty. I started to stand, in order to refill it, but he stopped me with a light hand on my forearm. "I know something weird is going on in this town, Twila, I've known as much as soon as I set foot here."

"I don't know—" I started, but then swallowed hard when I caught the expression in his eyes. He was warning me not to lie to him.

"The Osage people are people of belief," he started, looking at me in that way that made it feel like he was looking right through me. "And I was brought up to believe the stories and tales the elders would spin." He paused for a moment, making me wish he'd start talking again, just so I could enjoy the deep timbre to his voice. "While I believe in proof and science, Twila, I'm not arrogant enough to believe we, as humans, have all the answers—that we know the truth about life."

I swallowed hard. "It's good to be open-minded."

He nodded, but I could tell his mind was elsewhere. "As a child, I was told about the Osage wild people."

"The wild people?"

He nodded. "They can best be compared to fairies, I think. Anyway, the elders said they were one to two feet tall and sometimes they even had wings. They had magical powers and the elders warned that the wild people could be dangerous, sometimes kidnapping children or finding other ways to harm people."

I didn't know where he was going with this, but I was concerned about it, all the same. Not wanting him to witness the anxiety building in my eyes, I stood up before he could stop me and walked over to the kitchen counter to retrieve the glass bottle of moonshine. Then I walked back over to Dean and refilled his Mason jar when he gave me a quick nod. As soon as it was full, he reached down and swallowed two gulps full.

"When I was a little boy, maybe six or seven," he continued, wiping the alcohol from his upper lip onto his forearm. "I was in the forest, playing with one of my cousins," he continued and then breathed in deeply and his eyes settled on something in the distance—at the far end of the trailer. "And I saw one of these wild people."

I frowned. "You saw one?"

He nodded. "As clear as day—it had wings, just like the elders had said it might, and it was small—maybe a foot tall. It started to fly around us, as if watching what we were doing and my cousin got scared and ran off."

"And you didn't get scared?"

He chuckled as he shook his head. "No, I wanted to catch it."

"Of course, you did," I laughed along with him.

He took another sip of his moonshine. "But when I tried to catch it, I got this feeling. No, it was more than a feeling—it was like this knowledge, deep inside my mind, that it wasn't a good idea. It was this feeling that I was out of my element—that I was witnessing something I would never understand."

"Then you didn't try to catch it?"

He looked at me and shook his head. "No, I looked at it and it looked at me and there was this sort of understanding between the two of us and the thing flew away."

"Did you ever see it again?"

"No, never again."

"Wow," I answered, eyes wide. "You never told me that story before."

He chuckled. "It's not one of those things you willingly spread around because before you know it, your classmates start teasing you with stuff like 'Dean's seeing fairies'."

I laughed with him. "Do you believe that's what you really saw? A wild person?"

When he answered, his words were automatic. "Yes. I know what I saw." I lifted my eyebrows again, surprised to know this side of him existed. "And... there's a reason I'm telling you this, Twila."

"Is there?" I couldn't look at him and pretended to lose myself in my Mason jar instead.

"I know I saw a lizard man and a wolf man just now in the woods and I know I saw some sort of pig-looking man with tusks that day in the diner." He took a breath. "Just as I know I saw a wild person in the forest when I was a kid."

I didn't know what to say to that and so I didn't say anything at all. Instead, I just poured myself another jar of moonshine.

"And, what's more," Dean continued, staring at me even though I refused to look at him. And the weight of his stare—well, let's just say it felt like a semi-truck on my shoulders. "I know you know that what I saw was real."

I laughed at that, though I didn't know why I was laughing.

"I want to know the truth, Twila."

I looked up at him then and there was this dawning understanding within me—a realization that I couldn't keep the wool pulled over his eyes any longer—if it had really ever been pulled over his eyes, in the first place.

"The truth?"

He nodded. "I know you know what's really going on around here. You know the reason that half the town is gone—the reason why all the businesses are closed down. You know the reason why everyone who is left is avoiding me and you know the reason you've been doing your best to avoid me, as well."

"I haven't been avoiding you," I started.

He nodded. "You've been trying to keep me at arm's length—I'm no fool. I can feel it." I couldn't look at him and he must have noticed because he reached over and tilted up my chin with his fingers. "You've been trying to fight whatever this is between us."

I breathed in deeply. "What's between us?"

"The same thing that was between us twenty-three years ago," he answered and his tone was icy—as if he was daring me to argue with him. "You felt it just the same way I felt it."

I faced him squarely then. "And how do you know I feel anything?"

He smiled and I about melted right there. "When I kissed you."

I frowned. "What does that mean?"

"I could feel your true feelings in the way you kissed me—that's why I kissed you in the first place."

"What's why you kissed me in the first place?"

"So, I could get an idea of where I stood with you."

I frowned again. Damn him. "And where do you stand with me?"

"You want me just as much as I want you," he answered and that response made me think I needed a cold shower pronto. "But you're holding yourself back," he continued and not able to witness the smoldering in his eyes, I glanced down at the mason jar in my lap again. "And I want to know why you're holding back."

"I'm a single mom," I started, but he shook his head, interrupting me. When I looked at him, his expression was hard.

"Don't give me any of that crap. That's not why you're holding back—the real reason is something much bigger."

I realized I'd come to the end of the road—the end of the road where lying to Dean was concerned. At this point, there was moving forward. I'd have to either tell him I couldn't tell him the truth and hope he'd accept it (which I knew he wouldn't) or I'd have to just come out with it.

But I was scared to death to tell him the truth. Sure, he might have believed in fairies appearing to him as a kid in the forest, but this was different. This was bigger. This was heavier. This was... personal.

I suddenly felt the need to get some space and stood up, walking to the far side of the trailer. Then I found myself gazing out the window—into the dark forest just beyond the end of the road of River's Edge. Somewhere in that forest was a lizard man, a wolf man, a man who'd survived cancer and a hog-shifter that hopefully hadn't killed any of them.

"Twila?"

I turned back around to face the human who was sitting on my couch and staring up at me with a yearning expression in his eyes and I realized right then and there that Dean Hawke terrified me more than any bizarre creature I'd run into since the fog came.

"I need you to tell me the truth," he continued, voice even deeper. "Please, Twila."

The more I thought about letting him in on the secret, though, the more I worried about it. Not so much about what he'd do—I was fairly sure Dean wouldn't rat us out to anyone. No, he was a good man and he wouldn't want to see any of the residents in Windy Ridge meet bad ends. No, I was more worried for his own personal reaction to my news. What if, after finding out I was a vampire... what if he no longer felt attracted to me? What if he thought I was some kind of freak or, worse, what if he was petrified of me? What if he decided he wanted nothing more to do with me? What if he hated me for what I was?

"Twila," he said softly as he stood up and approached me, putting a hand on my shoulder.

"We don't really know what it was that killed the old sheriff," I started, swallowing hard as the words left my mouth. "But considering what state we found him in... it was probably some poor soul who went crazy when the fog rolled in and changed us into... whatever we are now."

Chapter Fifteen

Dean was quiet.

I could feel his eyes boring into the side of my face, but I couldn't look at him. For some reason, even though we were sitting here together and he was as flesh and blood as I was, looking at him just seemed like it made everything I'd just admitted too real.

"Whatever *you are now*?" he asked after a moment.

I sighed and shifted, taking another sip of moonshine just to feel the burn sliding down my throat. This was going to be the hard part—the part that made me wince when I actually thought about voicing it.

"Twila?" Dean continued, when I made no motion to continue.

I nodded and put my mason jar down. "A little over a year ago, something weird happened to

Windy Ridge and all the people in it. Well, not just here but in neighboring towns, as well."

"Okay."

"There was this fog that rolled in over the Ozarks, but it wasn't just your run-of-the-mill cloud cover. We still don't know what it was, but it was odd."

"Odd as in?"

"As in bright red and thick. Like the thickest fog you ever saw—and it was real low to the ground, like the fog you see in horror movies only imagine that bright red."

"Okay."

"Anyhow, it overtook the town in the span of an hour maybe." My hands were shaking. I could feel my heart tapping on my ribcage, rattling my spine and there was a sense of fear that was spiraling up inside me—making me want to pace the room. I held myself in check. "Once the fog spread through the town, people were different."

"Different how?"

I made the mistake of looking over at Dean and caught his narrowed gaze. I could only wonder what he thought of my story, but when I reminded myself that no matter how unbelievable it might sound, it was still the truth, I continued on. "Different as in everyone started to change into... well, into anything you can think of, really."

"Wolf men and lizard men, for example?"

I nodded. "Werewolves, fauns, devils, flying

things, badgers, rodents..."

"Hog men?"

I breathed in real deep then nodded. "It was like the town had become a children's horror story only real. Some of the folks couldn't take their new identities and just sort of lost their minds and disappeared into the woods. The rest of us just had to learn how to adapt."

Dean nodded and was quiet for a few moments as he focused on something in the distance and seemed to veg out. Then he took another swallow of his moonshine but didn't say anything more.

"That's why everyone's been avoiding you," I continued. "Some of them still look human like Boone, but most of them can't shift away from their new monster forms, and they didn't want you or Mason seeing what happened and notifying the authorities."

He looked at me then. "The government, you mean?"

I nodded and swallowed hard. "Yeah. You can imagine what would happen if any of us got found out."

He nodded. "It wouldn't be pretty."

"Right."

There was another long gap of silence between the two of us, during which I took a breath and found myself gazing out the window into the darkness. In the last few minutes of conversation with Dean, I'd sort of forgotten about the boys who were still out there. Even though I'd now told Dean the truth, I knew that if I said the boys were out there, trying to locate the hog shifter, he'd want in on the action. That was just owing to the fact of his job. And even though he seemed to be swallowing my story, that didn't mean I wanted to put his life in danger by getting him involved.

I glanced over at him and found his expression was stoic. He looked to be in full-processing mode as he took another long swig of the moonshine jar. "So, you're saying… this—this fog affected everyone?" He asked as I nodded. "And some of them were able to revert back to their human shapes? What about—" I thought this was going to the be the point where he asked after what I'd become and felt my breath catch at the thought of admitting what I was. "What about Deputy Drayton?"

I couldn't help the inward sigh of relief that flowed through me even if it was only momentary. Obviously, that line of questioning was going to come up sooner or later. "Merperson."

"Like a mermaid?" he frowned.

I shrugged again. "*Merperson* is the correct term."

"He doesn't have a tail," Dean pointed out.

I lifted my eyebrows at him. "Until he touches water."

Dean swallowed. "What about your friend, Boone? He looks human."

"He still is human."

"Then how's that work?"

"The fog seemed to have no rhyme or reason as

to what it did to all of us. Boone *was* terminal with cancer until the Fog came in. Not only did the fog appear to cure him, but it seems like he can't get sick at all. And he lost all his hair."

Dean chuckled at that. But then the laugh died on his lips and I could tell he was conflicted with the thoughts that must have been ramrodding his head. His brow creased with the strain to understand, and from the way he was looking at me, I was starting to worry he didn't believe me. There wasn't anything to do except to carry on, however, so I gave him an understanding nod and kept going.

"Anyway, that's why you haven't seen folks around. Most of us are scared that any normies—that's what we call regular folk like you and Mason—who find out are gonna sell us out to the FBI."

He nodded and then something seemed to occur to him. "Karen Dooley wanted to meet me the other day though?"

I nodded and breathed in real deep when I thought about that awful woman. "The only reason Karen contacted you is 'cause she wants to risk going back to the outside world, despite the rest of us fearing for our lives. And like I mentioned to you earlier, Karen isn't all quite there. Some days she seems to accept and understand what she is and other days she doesn't."

"And the mayor?"

"Is a hamster."

He shook his head and I could see the hint of a smirk on his lips. "I feel like I'm in a Monty Python skit."

"Well, much like it might feel that way, you aren't."

"Right."

"Right."

"So, the Lizard man and the wolf man I just saw in the woods?"

I was surprised he hadn't asked after me yet and figured he was just being considerate—allowing me to tell him my own story when I was ready. I appreciated that. "The lizard man is Ol' Ned," I started as Dean's eyes reached for the ceiling.

"Ol' Ned, huh? I wondered what became of that ol' coot."

"Yep, and the wolf man was Bud."

He chuckled at that. "Figures those two would keep on keepin' on, no matter what this strange world had in store for them." He looked over at me then. "And Slim Jim?"

I shook my head. "He's one of those who couldn't seem to manage and we don't know what became of him."

"I'm sorry to hear that," Dean said and glanced down at his mason jar. "I always liked that ol' hillbilly."

"Slim Jim was one of the sadder losses we've suffered." I took a breath. "But as to your question as to why Ol' Ned and Bud were out in the forest... well, they've become a sort of monster-hunting... team, I guess you could call them. They try to wrangle up the townsfolk who lost their minds." I took a breath, figuring this might be a good time to let him in on my own little secret. "And... most the time I help them."

"Wait, you've been self-policing?" Dean let a bit of surprise come into his voice.

"Well, with the old sheriff gone, we had to do something as a community," I answered, reaching up to rub my temple. "The only reason I got suckered into it is that I needed a fresh supply of... *food*." At Dean's expression—raised brows and obvious surprise, I quickly continued. "Well, that and I needed to keep Sicily out of trouble."

"Is Sicily a shifter then?"

I shook my head. "Luckily, she was at her pa's house when the fog rolled in, so for a while, she was the only human here—before you and Mason arrived."

"Then why do you have to keep her out of trouble?"

"She's gotten obsessed with trying to figure out what happened to all of us, but as smart as she is, I still don't wanna put her in harm's way. It's not safe work, keeping crazies from mauling the rest of the townsfolk to death."

"... So, aside from Ol' Ned and Bud... was that hog-man one of the 'crazies'?"

Somehow, I managed a smile as I shook my head. "I think so."

His brow furrowed. Dean looked at the moonshine and almost seemed ready to put it down, his head slowly shaking from side to side. "Twila, I don't... I don't know if I can..." He huffed, seemingly frustrated. "You know how crazy this sounds, right?"

"Of course, I do, but that doesn't mean it isn't the truth." This time, I fully turned to him and faced him with my tired eyes. "You believed in the wild people once upon a time, right?" He nodded. "Then is it so far-fetched to believe this too?"

He shook his head. "No, especially not when I remember what I've seen and I know it was real now as much as I did when I first saw it."

I breathed in real deep and figured my moment of reckoning had come. "You want proof?"

He looked up at me and swallowed hard.

"I won't hurt you," I continued, giving him an earnest look. "I can control the change."

He was quiet for another few seconds. Then he nodded. "I want to understand."

I breathed in real deep, then rolled up my sleeves, licking my tongue over the front of my teeth. Then I closed my eyes, willed myself to maintain the courage this was going to take and hooking my index finger around my top lip, I lifted it.

My lower jaw unhinged and I could feel the bones in my mouth begin to shift. Vampire anatomy, I'd found, was very strange. Kind of like snake fangs, my canines pressed inward towards my skull when I closed my mouth, and with the right amount of movement, I could make them slide out to their full two-inch length. It wasn't painful—it sort of felt like wiggling a loose tooth—but most of the time I kept the teeth well-hidden considering I didn't need to bite to feed. This time, though, I let them come out completely, and held my breath as I let Dean take a good look at them.

His eyes widened.

The air around us went deathly still as he leaned in for a better look, and when he moved away again, I let my mouth fall shut, bracing myself for his reaction.

"Wow." The word came out with a hush on his breath, and I couldn't tell if that was a good or a bad thing. "You... you weren't kidding."

"I wish I was," I said softly. "But, no. I'm not."

He was quiet for a few seconds but those seconds felt like years. Part of me expected him to down the moonshine in full—that's what *I* would have done—but instead, he tapped his fingers on the glass and looked at me, an oddly thoughtful gleam in his eye.

"Does it hurt," he asked. "Transforming into a..."

"Vampire."

He swallowed hard. "Vampire."

"No."

He smiled at me softly, unafraid, believing. I felt my heart jump and hesitated before putting my hand on his knee. "So, you believe me?"

"I don't see any other way," he replied with a chuckle and this time, he did reach down for his moonshine. "I mean. I saw a werewolf and a gigantic lizard running through the woods and you just showed me your fangs. At this point, I think I'd be an idiot not to believe you."

I nodded, but didn't feel like I was out of the woods yet. "And... do you feel okay with me? I mean... do you still feel the same?"

He looked at me and cocked his head to the side. "You're the same old Twila, right? I mean, except for obvious changes." Then he laughed again.

I nodded. "I'm the same person underneath it all."

He smiled and leaned in. "Then I still feel the same."

I gave him a smile of pure relief and, as he raised his jar again, clinked it against mine, we both took another painful gulp of the moonshine.

"Makes me wonder." He was mumbling a bit, and I could tell the drink was starting to settle in. "D'you know why Karen changed her mind about meeting me?"

"Oh." I made a face. "She didn't exactly change her mind. I just... *convinced* her not to meet you."

Dean raised his brow.

"It was for the sake of the community." I waved his look away. "She's one of the monsters and at that point in time, I couldn't let you see her, because I didn't—"

"Trust me."

I nodded. "I didn't know how you would react, Dean."

"I understand."

"What did she turn into?"

My mouth screwed into a knot. "Honestly?" I answered. "The devil."

Dean snorted. "How fitting." Then he shook his head and chuckled. "She was a devil of a woman when I knew her."

"Yeah, well now she's got the horns and tail to match. And she's bright red."

Dean shook his head. He was smiling, but I could tell it was a 'laugh or else you'll go crazy' type of smile, so I decided to quiet down and keep an eye on him as he processed. We sat for a few more minutes, pausing on the alcohol for the sake of our livers (not that mine minded), just stewing in the pile of information I'd just dropped. I felt foolish for it, but I was hopeful that things would be the same between us—that he wouldn't be afraid of me or keep me at arm's length owing to what I was.

As we looked at each other now though, Dean's expression wasn't harsh like the interrogator frown he'd given me when we spoken at the diner. His expression was much gentler now, almost resigned.

"Y'know," he said after another moment, "originally, I thought Windy Ridge was under a criminal ring's control. A cartel or something. With everyone avoiding me and evading questions, I figured you all were being threatened. But this... this is *way* more bizarre."

I sighed and clicked my tongue. "Yeah, you're telling me. And, y'know, I'm not gonna blame you if this is all too much for you. It was too much for *me* when it first happened, but you have the opportunity to leave—to go back to Branson. I just have to ask you though—if you do decide to turn tail…" I turned to him, then, face-to-face, "I need you to promise me that you won't tell anyone about us. These are good people, and even if *you* understand, I don't think many other people would. Would you swear to me that you'll keep this a secret?"

This time, I was the one burning holes in his face as I waited for his answer, my hands clenched and shaking with anticipation. Dean's eyes met mine and his frown deepened.

"I have no intention of leaving, Twila."

I don't know why but his words were a huge relief to me—maybe because I knew the chance of him letting the information out was less if he was living among us? But, no, my relief was because I wanted him to stay.

"You don't?"

He shook his head. "There's a distinct lack of law in Damnation County and there has been for a while." He put his hand on mine and his touch was cool. When I lifted my eyes to his, he broke into a smile. "I'm the sheriff here, and that means I need to take care of business."

My grin spread so wide, it hurt, and I squeezed his palm, shifting back to sit beside him. "Well, alright."

"But there is one thing I want you to promise me—since I promise you I will not tell another soul about what's going on in this town."

I swallowed hard. "Okay."

"I don't want you thinking I can't take care of sheriff business here," he answered, pretty astutely, if I did say so myself. "Even though I'm a human, I'm still the sheriff. And that means I don't want you keeping me in the dark any longer, Twila."

I thought about that. "These monsters can be dangerous."

"Humans can be dangerous."

I nodded and breathed in real deep when I looked at him. "I promise I won't keep you in the dark." And then I released the pent up breath of air. "And on that subject, we've got a shifter case to take care of."

Chapter Sixteen
The Next Day

Unfortunately, the boys had lost the trail of the shifter the night before and there hadn't been a sign of the nuisance since.

My hope was that the creature had simply moved on from Windy Ridge to terrorize Devil's Run or Dagwood. While that might not have sounded too neighborly, I was tired of having to deal with all the things that went bump in the night.

Being a bad neighbor or not didn't matter in the long run because the very next day there were sightings of the hog-man that started up again—apparently, he'd taken to rooting around in folks' trash. And, this time, the boys weren't shy about letting me know. Luckily, it wasn't until after my shift at the diner when they reached out.

"Twila?" Bud yelled into the phone once I picked it up.

"Yeah?"

"Word is the shifter hog's been spotted over at Battle Creek pass!" he yelled, panting which made me assume he was running. Where to or what from, I had no idea, but also didn't want to ask.

"Okay."

"You gonna tell that sheriff o' yours and meet us over there?"

"First off, the sheriff isn't 'mine' and secondly, yeah—"

But before I could continue, Bud was yelling over me, "I'm gonna shit my pants!"

And then the line went dead.

***

Once I got in touch with Boone (after figuring Bud was... *busy*), I learned I was supposed to get Dean and meet the boys by the treeline just behind River's Edge. From there, we were going to travel north to Battle Creek Pass and start our search.

Since I'd told Dean our little secret, so far, he'd kept to his word and kept it to himself. The only soul he'd told was his nephew (with my consent), and Mason hopped aboard the monster train faster than his uncle had, with an enthusiasm that reminded me far too much of my daughter's.

Regardless, now we were soon to face off with the so-called hog-man (at least, I hoped we were soon to face off with him), so I collected Dean, who collected Mason, who somehow managed to tell Sicily, who collected herself.

"How in the world did you even know where we were going?" I demanded of my daughter when I watched her walk up to join our crowd. We were currently standing in the clearing behind the trailer park and Ol' Ned was puzzling over a map he had sprawled out on an old picnic table, beneath one of the overhead lamps.

"I've been keeping in touch with the sheriff's nephew," she answered, giving Mason a sly smile as she walked up to stand beside him. I turned my angry glare on him and he immediately wilted.

"I'm sorry, Miss Twila, but Sicily told me you wouldn't be angry if she came along."

I frowned at both of them. "Well, she was wrong." Then I faced Dean and gave him the same perturbed expression. "I thought I just told *you* to come."

Dean shrugged and then smiled at me, holding up his hands in faux surrender. "I'm training Mason to be backup—eventually, I'd like to deputize him."

I frowned even further. "You already have a deputy."

"And two is better than one."

I frowned again but my bad temper didn't seem to matter so I quickly got over it. "Where is Deputy Drayton anyway?"

"He's manning the phones at the station," Dean answered. "We couldn't all go on this little adventure."

"Right." I'd sort of forgotten the fact that Dean still had a station to run.

"So, I can stay, Mama?"

I turned to look at the obvious hope in Sicily's eyes. "I thought you were supposed to be at home, doing homework?"

She nodded. "Well, I was until Mason texted me and told me what was going on. So... now I'm here." She took a deep breath. "And as part of the monster hunting team, I think it's important I'm included."

"I'll keep her safe, Miss Twila," Mason insisted.

I was spared the need to respond because Bud piped up instead. Shooting a glance at the sheriff, he looked back at me and with a cheeky grin asked, "You bit this one yet, Twila?"

I shot Bud a ferocious glare. Dean, meanwhile, looked over at me, wearing a strange expression—one I wouldn't exactly categorize as nervous, more curious, but I shook my head. Then I approached him and put a hand on his shoulder, still staring daggers at Bud's wide-open grin. "Ignore him. I don't bite people, and Bud knows that." Then I faced the werewolf and plopped my hands on my hips. "And you—can you hold it together for two minutes, for God's sake? I'm still not over the three of you aidin' and abettin' my kid's school absences."

Bud's ears pressed to his skull and his shoulders hunched. "Sorry, Twila."

"That's better." I sighed and stepped up, gesturing to the three monster hillbillies. "Dean, this is Bud and Ol' Ned in slightly... *different* forms," I started, even though it was weird to introduce them since they'd already known each other twenty-some-odd-years-ago. And, of course, I'd already let the boys in on the fact that the sheriff and his nephew were now in the know. They'd taken it better than I thought they would—their first question was whether or not the sheriff was now going to deputize the three of them. My answer was a hard no.

"Ol' Ned, Bud," Dean said and doffed his uniform hat. Both of them responded with statements along the line of *it's good to see you again.*

"I'm sure you remember Boone," I continued as the two in question said their hellos. "As you know Dean is now *Sheriff Hawke* of Windy Ridge and this is his nephew, Mason."

"Howdy." Bud's voice growled a bit as he raised a paw in greeting. Ol' Ned's reptilian face scrunched slightly, but he gave a polite nod in their direction.

"N-n-nice to see you again, Ossifer Hawke." Boone bowed slightly and smiled, the glow of the lamp overhead reflecting off his cue ball head. "Glad to have you on the t-t-team."

Dean looked them all over for a second or so, as if still trying to convince his mind that what his eyes were reporting was the God's honest truth. Then he simply smiled, though he did place a protective hand on Mason's shoulder.

"Thank you for letting us join you on this hunt," Dean started, looking at each and every one of us. "I plan to do everything I can to help catch this bastard."

"It's good to count you as one of us," Bud said and gestured to Mason. "And welcome to the team, Mr. Mason!"

"Well, they aren't exactly on the team," I started but everyone seemed to ignore me as Mason stepped forward and beamed.

"I'm real happy to be here, Mr. Bud."

"Mr. Bud!" Boone laughed as he slapped his hand on his thigh.

"You can just call me 'Bud', kid," the werewolf said with a wink.

"Okay, well the hog-man isn't waiting around for us to find him," I said, wanting to get to the point of the matter, because all this small talk was taking up too much time far as I was concerned.

"Right," Ol' Ned said. "I got word, not an hour ago, that the hog-man was rustlin' through the trash at the Jameson homestead."

"Then we gotta get us there!" Bud called out.

"And then do what with him?" I asked, frowning. "Do you have a trap set?"

"Summa bitch." Bud dropped his head. "Not yet."

I looked at Ol' Ned who nodded. "We thought the hog-man had moved on and just now got the call from Brother Jameson so we ain't had no time to fix up a trap."

"So?" I asked.

"So, we're gonna do this the ol' fashioned way," Ol' Ned answered.

And that meant I was going to have to wrestle the damned thing.

***

Sicily had begrudgingly agreed to wait in one of the old hunting towers that was just a few feet behind the trailer park and nestled in the woods. I'd left her a pair of binoculars and she'd brought her night-vision goggles so she could let us know if she saw the hog-man heading back towards the town.

Out of all of us, Bud was the best tracker in the group, so he was at the front, sniffing this and that as we stalked through the woods. Bud's tracking ability was owing to a mixture of his experience as a rifle hunter when he was human and his now acute sense of canine smell. If something was wounded though, no one could track it like I could. I could smell blood in the air from thirty feet away (I knew as much because Sicily had tested it). So far, though, I couldn't smell much beyond the scent of the damp woods.

But Bud could sniff out a frog in a swamp full of toads. He walked (on all fours) a few feet ahead of us with his nose stuck in the air while the rest of us kept a lookout from behind. Ol' Ned was directly behind Bud, carrying a rifle (which looked very bizarre when clutched by a lizard man) and Boone was walking just beside Ol' Ned, carrying his bowie knife.

The boys had made many a joke about Boone bringing a knife to a gunfight but it didn't seem to change the fact that Boone only liked to go on these monster missions when armed with his knife.

Dean had his pistol unsheathed and was glancing this way and that while Mason also carried a rifle, but seemed to be more infatuated with my less-than-human partners than he was with whatever was lurking in the woods. He kept asking Ol' Ned a ton of questions, and Ol' Ned responded with one-word answers. So, it was mostly me and Dean walking side-by-side with a joint combination of tension and nerves.

"So," Dean leaned over to whisper to me, his eyes locked warily on Bud who was still up ahead, pausing every now and again to angrily bite at a spot in his fur, just over his behind. "You've done this kind of thing before?"

"Many times," I replied. "It isn't too often we end up with something that's as hard to catch as this hog-shifter is proving to be, but it's happened before. I'm usually the one they send out to handle the real tough cases though."

"How come?"

"I'm the strongest," I said simply.

"Oh, is that so, wonder woman?" Dean smirked and I felt my skin prickle in a blush, so I nudged him in the side.

"Shut up," I answered on a laugh that was way

too close to a giggle for comfort. I quickly cleared my throat and regained my sensibility. "It's just a fact, sheriff. We haven't found anyone who can wrestle a monster like I can. And, believe me, we've been looking."

"Are all of these... what did you call them? Shifters?"

"Shifters, monsters," I answered on a shrug. "Crazies."

Dean laughed. "Crazies," he repeated as he shook his head. "Are they all as wild as the one we're dealing with now?"

"Not usually. Most the time they just act like what they are—people who have suffered a trauma and are mentally unstable because of it. These transformations weren't *nice,* you know? But once we actually catch them, since they were once human, I can usually talk them down from their hysteria in some way or another and we've had luck with reintroducin' them to the town. Well, that's just the human ones anyway."

"There are other types?"

I nodded. "When the fog came in, it changed not just humans but other animals too. So now the deer, bobcats, snakes, and coyotes are all sorts of strange creatures and they can be a bit more... *feral* to deal with."

"Feral as in?"

"As in non-thinkin'."

He nodded. "What have you done with the ones

—the feral creatures who were once forest animals—that you've already captured?"

"Well, mostly we've hunted them for food," I answered on a quick shrug.

"And you can tell the animals apart from those who were once human?"

I looked over at him. "Did that hog-shifter look more man or animal to you?"

"Man," he answered without a pause.

I nodded. "Right. Those who were once human are easy to recognize because they still look human, more or less."

"How do you introduce them back into the population once you catch them?"

"We sort of rehab those who want to try and adapt to normal life." I took a breath and kept my gaze on Bud, who was still tracking the scent of what I supposed was the hog-shifter up ahead. "We introduce them back to Windy Ridge slowly, and most of the townsfolk help us out when we do. Everyone wants the opportunity to find a loved one they lost."

"And those you can't rehab?"

I looked over at him. "We actually haven't come across one yet. The humans usually take a couple of days, maybe a week, to remember what it means to be civilized. And the rest of the monsters we've caught were animals before the fog found them."

"And what about this shifter?" Dean continued. "The hog-man. You think he's still... sentient?"

I breathed in real deep because it was a question

I'd already asked myself repeatedly. "I don't know," I answered finally. "This one could be too far gone."

"What do you do with him then?"

I looked over at him and smiled. "I think we turn him over to the sheriff."

Before Dean could respond, something rang through the air—a high-pitched, throaty squeal, and a shout very closely following.

"Incoming!"

We turned.

On pure instinct, I grabbed Dean's arm and jerked him out of the way, cringing as I worried I might have pulled too hard and injured him. Meanwhile, the hog-man sprinted past us. It was on all fours and skidded to a halt before it rammed into a tree and then bouncing off the trunk, glared around itself, madness glinting in its tiny, pig-like eyes.

Dean gathered himself enough to pull out his pistol as I whipped around to face Bud. "What the *hell,* why didn't you say it was that close?!" I yelled, ushering Mason over towards his uncle.

"'Cause I didn't *know* it was so close!" Bud shouted back, clearly distressed. "There's hog smell all over these woods, and I was tryin' to hone in on the person part of it, but there's hardly any!"

Dean aimed his gun but didn't fire—it was dark, and there were too many people around to risk taking a shot he wasn't sure he could hit. I saw his eyes dart side-to-side and then I caught a flash as the hog-man came out of seemingly nowhere, running hell-bent for Dean. Without thinking, I threw myself into Dean, knocking him over as the beast just missed the two of us.

"Bud! Boone—go after it!" I yelled as I pulled myself up to standing and reaching down, offered Dean a hand. He took it and then the two of us were off, chasing the two hillbillies who were running after the hog-man.

I wasn't sure where Ol' Ned was.

Chapter Seventeen

Turned out, we'd lost the hog-man yet again.

After the near run-in with Dean, we'd decided to head back to the trailer park (picking up Sicily along the way) to regroup.

"This thing's smarter than we realized," Ol' Ned said as he paced the dirt road out front of his trailer. The rest of us stood around him in a circle like we were schoolkids at show-and-tell. "We're gonna need us a trap."

I could have told him that from the get-go but decided not to say as much. Instead, I folded my arms and looked towards him and the blueprint-sized paper he'd unfurled on top of the picnic table that stood beside his double-wide in the field at the end of River's Edge. "Are you sticking with the old trap or are we gonna have to make a new one?"

Ol' Ned gave a thoughtful sniff and looked out

at the field in front of him. The boys had set up some portable tables and chairs for a makeshift workshop out there, though most of their supplies were scattered all along the ground. The boys definitely weren't any good at organization.

"Lil'a both." He turned the blueprint towards me and pointed to the diagram. "We're fixin' to replace the net with a cage so the squirrely thing don't hurt itself, but last time we tried to catch that coyote-bear, the danged thing leapt clear over the trigger string. An' I bet this hog-shifter's smart enough to do the same."

"So?" I asked.

"So, we'll need'a put that trigger higher and find a better way to cover it, 's well as put some fail safes in place to make sure we catch the dang thing."

"We're also g-g-gonna add some tranquilizing darts." Boone smiled eerily and motioned to a few vials on the table. "C-c-cause it seems to be a rowdy one."

"You're gonna tranq it?" I asked in disbelief as I shook my head. "Need I remind you that tranqs aren't gonna work on shifters? You know that!"

"This'n does," Ol' Ned said, turning back to the blueprint. I stared at him blankly and Bud sighed, scratching behind his ear with his massive back leg. I could only wonder if he had fleas.

"Most chemicals don't work on us, right enough," Ol' Ned said. "But that don't mean they do *nothin'*. Brother Bud had him the wise idea to try somethin' stronger and a little less... *safe* to see if it might have a drowsy effect on the beast."

I felt my right eye twitch. "Ned," I said slowly, "what's in those vials?"

Ol' Ned sniffed again. "Cyanide."

I felt my heart about drop out of my chest. "Where did you get Cyanide?"

"D'you really wanna know?" Ol' Ned raised his lizard brows at me and then made a point to look at the sheriff, like he didn't trust the lawman.

"Hey, I understand that roundin' up shifters is a whole different ball game than I'm used to," Dean said as he faced Ol' Ned. "As long as you can tell me that whatever you're plannin' won't kill the thing—"

"It ain't gonna kill 'im," Ol' Ned responded.

Dean nodded. "Then I say you've gotta do what you've gotta do."

I pursed my lips because I wasn't convinced. I'd seen these boys come up with some pretty outlandish inventions in the past and to say they hadn't been pretty was an understatement. On one occasion it had involved an explosion and lots of fire...

"Don't worry, darlin', it'll be right fine," Bud said easily, though his wolfish grin was a little guilty. "The cyanide will just knock that hog-man out, like any normal tranq would."

"How do you *know?*" I whipped around to face Bud, and the guilt spread even more so across his face.

"We may have... *tested* it a 'lil."

"We tested it all right and Brother Bud was out for three hours." Ol' Ned gave a loud, hissing laugh. "'N that was only one vial."

"And let me guess where you got the idea to use one vial on Bud," I continued, as I turned to face my daughter.

She shrugged. "Hey, I told them one vial wouldn't kill him and I was right!"

I just rubbed the bridge of my nose, shaking my head. "If I don't end up killing the lot of you one day, apparently you'll do it for me."

Bud chuckled, and Ol' Ned's reptilian eyes turned to Dean, who I could tell was trying not to laugh. "You. Sheriff. You got any skill with wrenches?"

Dean jolted a bit, surprised. "Uh... Yeah, actually. I used to fix up old cars before I joined the force."

"Good." Ol' Ned glanced over to Mason. "An' you, Brother Mason?"

"I'm a fast learner." Mason grinned.

"Fine by me." Then Ol' Ned walked over to the table and flicked his green, scaly and clawed 'index finger' at the blueprint. "Yer gonna wanna take off that pretty shirt'a yours, Mr. Police. Things about to get downright greasy."

Dean gave me a fleeting look of apprehension before he and his nephew followed Ol' Ned out to the yard which was so littered with mechanical debris, it looked like a bomb had gone off. I turned to face Bud, who was on all fours, scratching and biting at that spot above his rear end. "For the love o'

Pete," I started, shaking my head. "Do I have to get you some flea spray?"

Bud looked up and cocked his wolf head in my direction as his hind leg continued to scratch his itch. "I dunno if I got them fur critters, Twila, but summa bitch do I gotta itch!"

"I'm g-g-gonna keep a ear out for the creature j-j-just in case." Boone clapped me on the shoulder and then gave me a knowing expression though I wasn't sure why.

"Okay."

Then Ol' Ned looked up at me. "Can you take Sugar Plum an' try'n find us a good place to put the trap and set up the trail cameras?"

I glanced at Sicily and frowned. "Let's go scouting."

"Can I tag along?" Mason asked, but faced Sicily instead of me.

"Sure can," she answered as she walked over to Ol' Ned and picked up the metal trail camera case. As long as the cameras were all working, we had three we could strap to nearby trees in order to keep a visual on the trap, in case we failed to catch the shifter.

"We'll need to locate a dense area in the woods where a trap could be easily hidden," I informed them as we started for the tree line.

"But not so dense that the hog-man can't get through," Sicily added with a quick nod.

We easily caught up to Boone and he walked

beside Mason. "I hear you g-g-got you some talent when it c-c-comes to sketchin'?"

"Oh," Mason started.

"He's really, really good," Sicily agreed.

"Then I'm hopin' we c-c-can convince you to join our little team here," Boone continued. "We c-c-could use them artistic skills o' yours to g-g-get drawins o' our eye-witness accounts."

"Boone," I warned. "Don't be annoying."

Mason laughed. "I'd be happy to help you guys out." Then he took a big breath. "Sicily's told me about some of the things you've caught and I'd definitely like to help any way I can."

Most of my attention was on my daughter as I side-eyed her. She was standing next to me, but her attention was fully focused on Mason, and I saw a very familiar look of infatuation in her eyes. That put me on edge probably more than it should have; she'd been isolated from the rest of the world for a year, and the only people her age were various monsters down at Dagwood High.

I guessed I shouldn't have been surprised she'd taken such a quick liking to Mason. She probably would have been fascinated with him even if he wasn't carrying on the Hawke family's especially good looks. I made a mental note to sit down with Mason if things started to progress and the two of them actually started dating, but for now, I tried to push the worry aside. We had bigger things to worry about than a mother's concern for her daughter's love life.

***

Finding a good place for a trap was surprisingly fairly simple.

We locataed a nice glen with thick underbrush that could hide the tripwire Ol' Ned was planning on using. Meanwhile, I tested a couple of nearby trees by pulling on the branches in order to see if they were sturdy enough to handle a hog-man. If the branches could handle vampire strength, then the weight of one shifter ought to be a piece of cake.

Meanwhile, Sicily and Mason set to securing the trail cams to three surrounding trees. As to how we were going to lure the hog-man into the trap? Food. That was always the ticket when it came to catching monsters. They were one hungry lot and a nice, rare, and bleeding steak was usually just the thing.

The rest of the boys and Dean were hard at work when we got back. Ol' Ned was overseeing the project, barking orders in his raspy voice, and Bud and Dean were the ones doing the constructing. Actually, Dean was doing most of the constructing because Bud kept pausing to scratch himself. I'd have to see about getting him some flea powder right quick.

Sicily and I reported our findings to Ol' Ned and then focused on the next piece of business— Sicily was to be in charge of setting up a command base where she could keep an eye on the trail cameras (I'd figured this was the safest job for her since

I definitely didn't want her out in the field). And that command base was going to take place just outside Ol' Ned's trailer—on the porch underneath the overhang, overlooking the field. My job, meanwhile, was going to be helping to wrangle the creature in case the trap failed. And although Ol' Ned was good at designing traps in general, it wasn't unusual for them to fail.

Until then, I sat myself on a nearby rock and watched the construction process. Boone and Mason both walked over to Dean and Bud in order to lend a hand. I didn't mind taking myself a respite because it meant I got to look at Dean while he worked. I don't know what was coming over me lately, but something where that uniformed man was concerned definitely was. Now, I took the opportunity to admire the fit figure he kept hidden underneath his uniform. I was a simple woman (well, for a vampire, anyway), and I wasn't going to apologize for enjoying seeing a man lift a heavy thing once in a while.

What I *did* mind, however, was the look on my daughter's face when I glanced over at her and found she was doing the same thing I was—admiring a Hawke as she stood on Ol' Ned's porch and glanced out at the field with a real dreamy expression on her face. Only her eyes weren't on Dean, but on Mason, who was working beside his uncle diligently. And the expression on Sicily's face—well, it was like she was looking at Mason like he was a thick slab of icing on the last slice of cake. Breathing out a big, long sigh, I had to actively push down my motherly instinct to reach over and cover her eyes.

"Aren't you supposed to be paying attention to setting up your command center?" I asked her pointedly and then pointed to the plastic table in front of her and her laptop computer (a gift from her father) which looked like it still wasn't plugged in or turned on. "Instead, it looks like you're paying way too much attention to Mason Hawke."

She giggled. "Well, do you really blame me, Mama? He's the best lookin' guy to come this way in a long time."

I couldn't argue that, so I didn't even try. I did, however, walk over to Ol' Ned's porch and wrapped my fingers around the wooden railing. Sicily glanced toward me with a smile plain on her face.

"I'm sorry if I'm overstepping, but maybe it isn't a good idea to get attached." I said in a real soft voice as she raised her brow at me, obviously confused.

"What? Why?"

"Well, we have no idea how long they're gonna stick around after—" I looked back and took in the lizard-man who was barking orders at a werewolf and two humans. And Boone. I sighed. "After this."

"Sheriff Hawke made it pretty clear he had no interest in leavin' I thought?"

I breathed in real deep, then pursed my lips and looked at Dean again with a tug in my gut. "I just don't want you to get your hopes up too much, that's all." And the same went for me, though I didn't want to acknowledge it as much—not to Sicily and not even to myself.

Sicily hummed and then shrugged, folding her arms over her chest as she reached down and plugged her laptop cord into Ol' Ned's outdoor outlet which was already piled with cords—so many that the thing was an absolute fire hazard.

"I dunno. I've got a good feeling they'll stay."

I scoffed without realizing it. "Why do you say that?"

She looked at me with that big smile of hers. "Well, they seem pretty happy here and what's more—Sheriff Hawke seems pretty invested."

"He'd be invested in his job no matter where he was."

She shook her head and that grin of hers grew. "That's not what I meant."

"Then what did you mean?"

"That he's invested *in you*, Mama."

My face went bright red. Sicily snickered as I checked to see if Dean had overheard her, but he was still about ten feet away, rooting through the field, no doubt looking for some part he wasn't going to have an easy time finding. When I looked back at my daughter, she was already retreating, yelling about needing the restroom before she disappeared into Ol' Ned's trailer.

Chapter Eighteen

It wasn't much longer before the boys had managed to get a trap made and after another hour or so, it was set and ready to go.

That was when we got a phone call from Jebediah Gibson at the far end of town. Apparently, he'd heard a ruckus coming from his barn and when he went to investigate, he found a pink man, covered in bristles, with tusks coming from his bottom jaw eating his goat feed.

"Summa bitch! That's miles from our trap!" Bud complained.

"Ain't a whole lot we can do about that now," Ol' Ned answered as he popped a few TUMS, then made for his old Chevy pickup. Dean and I were already behind him and Sicily was manning the cameras in her control center, even though I doubted the hog-man would find his way back to our trap when he was currently at the opposite end town.

"Thing is movin' f-f-fast," Boone said as he piled in beside Ol' Ned and Bud piled in beside him.

Dean opened the door to his police cruiser for me and Mason took a seat in the back. Then we were off and following Ol' Ned to the other side of town.

After a good ten minutes, we arrived at Jebediah's ranch.

"What in the hell is that?" Dean asked as we pulled into the driveway and the highlights of his cruiser lit up Jebidiah, who was waiting for us just beside his barn.

"That's Jebediah," I answered.

"He's a—" But Dean lost his words.

"Centaur," I answered.

"Right," Dean responded with a quick nod as he put the cruiser into park.

"I seen him disappear 'round the back!" Jebediah called out when I opened my door and stepped out. The boys were already out of Ol' Ned's truck and standing in front of Jebediah who turned and pointed at the woods behind his barn.

"Sweet molasses! How long ago he take off?" Ol' Ned called out.

"Oh, shit, maybe right before you boys got here."

And then Ol' Ned was off, running as fast as his lizard legs and long tail would allow him as Bud took the lead, running on all fours and pausing here and there to sniff the air. Boone took up the rear and

Dean, Mason and I easily caught up with him.

We moved quickly through the forest and I could hear the heartbeats of everyone around me—they were pounding. We all stopped running when Bud stood up and turned around, his nose in the air. He did a full circle before facing the rest of us.

"The scent stops here," he announced.

Just then, I heard the distinct sound of snorting and a moment later, the underbrush shifted under the furious stampeding sound of hooves. There was a flash of pink in the moonlight and another grunting sound and then I heard gunfire, though I wasn't sure who had fired the shots.

The flash appeared again, this time coming right for Mason, so I grabbed his shoulders with both hands and spun him, bracing as the fleshy, but hard surface of the shifter's head crashed into my ribs. I went flying and the thing's tusks stabbed through my shirt, digging into my skin but luckily, I managed to grab hold of them to keep the thing from running me all the way through as we both fell.

"Twila!" I heard both Bud and Dean scream as I was hit. My jaw was clenched tightly to keep the damn thing from escaping as the hog-man punched and kicked at my torso. I wrestled it like an alligator, trying to wrap my legs around its head to keep it still, but it was squirming so violently, I was half-afraid it would rather snap its own neck than be subdued.

"Somebody *get* this thing!" I shouted, and out of

the corner of my eye, I saw Dean turn.

"Ned!" he called. "Get me some of those tranquilizers!"

"On it!" I heard Ol' Ned start frantically patting his torn blue overalls just as the shifter flipped me, slamming me back-first into a nearby boulder. "Dadgummit," Ol' Ned continued to mumble. "I had one in here somewhere—"

Meanwhile, Bud dove for the thing but missed, ramming his big wolf head into the trunk of a nearby tree.

"I gotta shot I can take!" Mason yelled as I looked up and saw him aiming his rifle at the two of us.

"Don't shoot!" Dean screamed at him. "You'll hit Twila!"

"Ned!" My scream was hoarse, half my air getting knocked out of me from the impact with the thing. And, as far as I could tell, the hog shifter had found some mud to roll in because he was literally caked in it and as we wrestled, more and more began to flick off all over me.

Finally, Ol' Ned lifted a syringe out of his back pocket and Dean grabbed it from him. But just as he ran over to stab the shifter, it kicked its feet back, landing Dean square in the legs. Dean grunted, stumbled, and I felt my stomach drop as the syringe shattered on the rock beside my head.

"Shit!" Dean yelled, and rolled as the shifter kicked at him again, barely missing landing a hoofed foot to Dean's eye. I was sweating by this point, and my grip was beginning to slip off the shifter's slobbering tusks. Instead of letting it trample me, I yanked it as hard as I could, letting go briefly in order to shove a finger into its eye. The thing squealed out in pain, we rolled, and I all but scrambled towards the rest of the group. Bud reached for my arm and yanked me to my feet.

"Summa bitch is *crazy!*" He panted, lips snarling instinctively. "I ain't never seen one like it!"

"We need to lead it back to the trap, brother Bud!" Ol' Ned yelled from behind. "We gotta lure it down, come on!"

"There's no way we can lure this thing all that way! Whoever it is, they're outta their *mind!*" I shouted back as I pushed the hair out of my face.

My jab to the hog-man's eye had staggered it, but the damned thing didn't seem to want to let up anytime soon. It was still huffing and puffing, never stopping for more than a moment's breath before charging one of us again. Whoever this was—it was out for blood.

It went for Bud again. I was ready to tackle it, knowing it was probably fruitless if we didn't have the trap to hold it in, but Bud put an arm in front of me and spread his legs until they were shoulder width. Then as soon as the shifter was close, Bud bent down and let out the loudest, most chilling roar I'd ever heard. The shifter scrambled and veered right, not stopping and instead, changing its course.

Directly for Dean.

Pistol out, Dean fired. He missed. The hog-man's weaving was making it impossible to keep aim on the damned thing. Dean fired again, and the sound spooked the thing, but still, the bullet missed it.

I was sprinting in their direction at the exact same moment that Mason put his hands on Dean's shoulders and shoved him out of the way of the shifter.

I screamed. I wasn't the only one; Bud let out another howl, this time in shock, and Dean's voice was almost as agonized as Mason's as the creature's tusk dug bone-deep into Mason's shin. Then it ripped upward, trampling its way overtop Mason, and only then was Dean able to aim, fire, and hit the damned thing in the side.

The hog-man shrieked and sped off into the woods, bleeding. I could smell the blood as clearly as if someone had sprayed perfume right into my face. I didn't rush after the damned thing though, because I knew I could track it now that it was injured. And besides, I didn't care enough to traipse after it at the moment. Instead, I raced to Mason's side as Dean helped him up to a seated position. Mason's eyes were wide and I could tell by the expression on his face that he was in a lot of pain.

Dean grabbed his hand. I brushed the hair out of Mason's face and felt my stomach roll at how pale he looked already. "Hey, *hey*. Mason?"

"*Agh,*" Mason squeezed his uncle's hand. Tears pearled in the corners of his eyes. "S-sorry, I'm sorry—I, I didn't want you to get hurt, I didn't mean—"

"I'm fine and that's only because of you," Dean answered as he leaned forward and reaching down, ripped a piece of material from the bottom of his shirt. Then he fashioned a tourniquet around the top of Mason's wound.

I turned over my shoulder. Bud and Ol' Ned were hurrying towards us. Facing forward again, I looked down, into Mason's eyes, but before I could speak, I inhaled and instantly my heart went *wild*.

I hadn't smelled human blood this close ever. And the moment I did, the moment that scent hit my nostrils, I knew my being this close to Mason was bad. I had to get away from him.

"Dean." I stood up and stepped away, angling my head towards the direction where the shifter had disappeared. "Bud and Ol' Ned can help you get Mason back to town—he needs to have that wound seen to. I'm gonna start tracking this thing and see if I can't knock it out cold."

I didn't say it out loud, but in my head, I was ready to kill this thing. It may have been a person at one point, but as far as I was concerned, it wasn't any longer. Now, it was a danger to the rest of us. I wasn't going to *try* to kill it, but if that was the only way I'd be able to stop it? Well, I wasn't known for being squeamish.

"Be careful, Twila," I heard Dean say. I didn't dare look at him for fear of getting another whiff of Mason's blood, but I nodded, licked my teeth, and ran away faster than I ever ran before.

***

Normally when I was on a chase, I was focused, keeping my wits about me in case whatever I was looking for was going to jump out or charge me. But this time, everything felt a little more... 'natural' for lack of a better word.

My muscles almost moved of their own accord, pumping powerfully and without strain. I felt like I could see better, like the shadows of the trees were sharper, making it easier to dodge them. I could see the blood trail on the leaves of the trees as well as the ground, glistening slightly in the moonlight. But even if I hadn't been able to see it, I could scent it—thick and potent in the night air.

As I moved as quickly as my vampiric speed would allow me, I vaulted over a log in my path and landed in a crouch, putting my head low to the ground. Inhaling very slowly, I allowed every bit of the shifter's blood scent to fill my head. When I opened my eyes, the blood on the leaves before me seemed to glow even brighter.

I almost felt like an animal, like I was a predator tracking its prey. And strangely, maybe just in that moment, I was perfectly alright with that.

I sped off again. Over rocks, over brush, through small creeks, and over fallen logs. When I shoved a branch aside, I almost felt like I could propel myself forward if I wanted to—like I could grab onto a branch and swing upward, leaping tree to tree like a squirrel. That feeling was strangely intoxicating, weirdly powerful.

The blood started to smell fresher, stronger. And that meant I was gaining on the damned thing.

I smirked and rounded the corner of a grove of trees, but as soon as I did, I instantly dug my heels into the dirt, skidding a few feet before I stopped.

There weren't many things I was surprised about these days. Over the past year, I'd seen folks I'd grown up with eating raw flesh, others growing wings and flying off, never to be seen again. Something I didn't expect, however—something I *never* would have expected—was to see a cabin with an attached garden, both nicely taken care of, hidden this deep in the woods.

It wasn't a large place. One of those one-room-plus-an-outhouse type homes. It wasn't painted either, but the walls and the windows were clean which was more than I could say for most folks' residences in town. As I looked up, panting, I could see smoke rising from the little stone chimney perched on its roof.

I was so baffled, I had to take a step back, trying to understand who could be living out here, in the middle of a monster-infested forest. And better yet, how had we never stumbled on this place before now? When all of this fog nonsense started, we'd assumed that anyone sane had gravitated toward one of the three affected towns, and the rest had simply lost their minds and were still roaming the forests.

Apparently, we were wrong.

The cabin was still a few hundred feet away from me and I felt a bit hesitant to approach it, but there was a good chance that whoever was inside it had seen where the hog shifter had gone. What was more, it was my responsibility to let them know the thing was close and it was dangerous.

Slowly, I made my way towards the front of the cabin, but the closer I got, the more I could smell blood—the same scent I'd been tracking. I looked down and noticed that the blood trail I'd been following led directly to the cabin, up the wooden porch steps, across the porch and ended at the front door. Creeping closer, I noticed a high-pitched whining coming from behind the front door.

Before I could so much as reach the bottom step of the porch, the front door of the cabin opened, and I was met with the shine of a shotgun barrel aimed right between my eyes.

I stopped in time, but barely.

The hog-man had scuttled inside the warm-looking cabin, its whimpering even more audible now that the door was open. My eyes were locked on those two barrels and I felt the fight drain out of me like someone had pulled a plug from my sternum.

Vampires were strong, but I didn't think I could survive a head full of buckshot. And it was really something I didn't want to test out.

"I'm not here to hurt you," I started as I realized something—I was about to be shot full of bullets out here, in the middle of nowhere and no one would know what had happened to me. I was about to die, and not one person would have a clue as to where I'd gone or what had happened.

What a stupid way to go.

In the silence that lasted for what felt like minutes, I heard the holder of the gun breathe in. The barrel dipped slightly, and then dropped.

"Well, feck me, Miss Twila? Izzat you?"

I managed to swallow, despite my dry mouth and slowly lifted my eyes. The speaker was a shifter, I knew that much instantly; he had a rodent snout and bristly fur covering his arms, almost like a beaver or a muskrat, but the human parts of him were thin and gangly. His clothes looked clean but well-worn, as if they'd been repaired by hand many times. And his eyes were bright blue, staring at me in awe and realization.

I took a step back, my hands hanging loosely by my sides, because I knew those blue eyes.

"Slim Jim?"

Chapter Nineteen

Before I could so much as utter another word, I heard the sound of footsteps and turned to see Bud, Boone, Ol' Ned, and Dean walking up behind me.

Apparently, they'd been trying to follow me ever since I'd run off, but were very nearly lost thanks to the thickness of the forest brush.

Once he walked up beside me, Dean explained that Sicily had taken Mason in Dean's cruiser to the Spider House for medical attention. The Spider House was the closest thing we had to a clinic and was run by a half-woman, half-spider who in her human days had been a nurse. She was still a master at stitches (only now she simply created her own webbing stitches). Even though the gash was an ugly one, Dean didn't believe it was life-threatening so there was that.

Now, we had another mystery to solve and we all hesitantly approached the cabin. Slim Jim was still standing there, looking at us like things were just fine and he hadn't been missing all this time. The glow of the fireplace backlit him as we approached.

Dean and I walked up beside him, but Bud, Ol' Ned, and Boone were standing by the porch stairs, staring up at him in awe. When you looked at him right, Slim Jim was still in his new body somewhere. The bulbous nose had just been turned into large a muskrat snout, and he still had his long white, snowy beard that about reached his navel. He had that same edge of warmth to his expression even when staring suspiciously at the three figures standing below him. I watched as his eyes fell on Boone, whose ghostly face smiled a bright and shining grin.

"… J-J-Jim." Boone gave a breathless laugh. "It's really you."

"Well, I'll be feckin' damned." Slim Jim pointed to Boone. "Ain't you 'sposed to be dead?"

Boone laughed again. "The fog didn't do everyone a d-d-disservice, friend."

Slim Jim smiled. "Well. Ain't that feckin' something,' Boonie."

"Slim Jim," Bud said, stepping forward slightly and putting one of his paw-hands on his chest. "D'you remember me?"

Slim Jim narrowed his eyes and looked Bud up and down. "Don't reckon I knew a dog feller in my time."

"It's me," Bud insisted and I could hear the crack in his voice. "It's Bud." Then he bit his lip and patted Ol' Ned's scaley back.

"An' I'm Ol' Ned, brother Jim." He breathed in like he was getting sentimental. "From River's Edge. From before."

I watched Slim Jim start in surprise, obviously not recognizing Bud or Ol' Ned. He looked to and from the monsters standing before him and, when Bud started to climb the stairs, Slim Jim didn't back away. Bud reached into one of his pants pockets and pulled out a worn photograph that I could just see over Slim Jim's shoulder; it was a picture of the four of them, holding up their game, a smile forever encapsulated in time.

"It's us," Bud said again as he handed Slim Jim the photo. "I carry this around in remembrance of you."

Slim Jim stared at the photo. Then he took it from Bud's hand with his furry paw and looked from it to them to it again. His eyes started to water, and as he stepped back to see them in full, Slim Jim let out the loudest, happiest holler I'd heard in months and sprinted full-force into a massive group hug.

They stayed like that for quite a while, mumbling at each other with laughter and tears galore and a few 'feckings' thrown in, until eventually Slim Jim extracted himself and invited us inside.

He gave me a quick hug which I returned. Even though we were happy to see each other, Slim Jim had always been closest with the boys. They'd grown up together so I supposed it followed.

We walked into the one-room house (it's not true what they say about vampires needing to be invited in) and saw that the outside of the cabin matched the inside in that it was clean, save for some dishes on the table or the unmade bed. The only off-color thing though was the cage by the kitchen and the crouched, pitiful-looking hog-man now locked inside it. The thing locked eyes with me when I walked in and whimpered, and part of me was almost calm enough to feel bad for it, with its side all patched up in gauze and medical tape. Still, it was a pain in my ass. And one I needed an explanation for.

"Well, feckin' sit yerselves down an' I'll get us somethin' to take off the shock." Slim Jim motioned to the center of the room, where a shabby couch and chair were placed by a bookshelf, and then paused, glancing and counting the number of people. That was when he noticed Dean. "Who the feck are you?"

So, I introduced them and before long, Dean was as welcome in Slim Jim's house as the rest of us.

Bud plopped himself right on the ground while Dean and I took the couch, Ol' Ned crawled into the chair with a flick of his lizard-tongue. "So how you manage to live out here, in the middle of the woods, Brother Jim?" Then he glanced out the window at the garden which was showcased in the moonlight.

"And who in tarnation's garden is that?"

"Mine," Slim Jim replied, grinning as he put a kettle on to boil. There was a working wooden stove in the kitchen, as well as bags of vegetables and grain leaning against the side of the counters. "Grew it m'self. If you got the right eye fer it, you can find all sorts'a seeds in them there feckin' woods, I tell you."

"How long you *been* out here?" Ol' Ned rasped. "We been lookin' for your sorry ass for a whole damned year!"

"That's right," Bud added on a nod. "We been lookin' from here to Dagwood right down to Devil's Run and we didn't find no *trace*."

To that, Slim Jim let out a high-pitched prospector's laugh and shrugged. "Since that danggon red stuff passed through, 'course! I thought I was the only one who didn't go'n lose my feckin' mind 'cause o' it. After this happened," he raised his hands, gesturing to his thick fur and bucked teeth, "I didn't wanna wait 'round for no FBI agent to come wanderin' into Windy Ridge, ready to slap me on a table like feckin' sushi."

Then he looked over at Dean like he was worried Dean was that exact FBI agent.

"I'm not FBI," Dean answered, holding up his hands.

"Well, good for feckin' you!" Slim Jim responded as he then faced the rest of us. "Hells bells, I nearly blew Miss Twila's head right off'er feckin' shoulders when she showed up here. Thought she was an agent'er the tax man or somethin'." Slim

Jim gave me a guilty grin and I just frowned at him. "Sorry 'bout that, by the way, darlin'. Can't never be too feckin' careful 'round here."

"No harm done." I waved him off, even though I'd be thinking of that shotgun barrel for the next few days to come, if not for the rest of my life. "And you're not the only one with that worry. The whole of Windy Ridge's been closed off from everywhere outside Damnation County all year."

Slim Jim let out a long whistle. "Is that feckin' so? Dang shit spread that far?"

"Everywhere from here d-d-down to Devil's Run," Boone answered.

"Maybe further," I added. "Hard to say. We're only in contact with those other towns at the moment."

"So's theres more'a ya?" Slim Jim asked, excitement growing in his eyes. "Y'all ain't the only ones with yer mind's about ya?"

"Windy Ridge lost about a third of its population from what I can gather," Dean said, "but there are plenty of folks just like you back there."

"An' what the feck kinda creature are you, lawman?"

"I'm a sheriff."

Slim Jim frowned at him. "What you turn into?"

"I have two guises—sheriff and off-duty sheriff," Dean answered with a smile as I shook my head. Hillbillies tended to be literal sorts so he wasn't doing himself any favors.

"He's human," I supplied with a frown at Dean. At that moment he got a text and glancing down at his phone, looked up again. "That's Sicily. She said they arrived at the Spider House and Edna is stitching Mason up right now. He'll be fine."

"Edna?" Slim Jim repeated, a smile taking hold of his features. "She still alive?"

"An' kickin'," Bud answered.

I nodded, figuring we had some explaining to do, just as he did. "We've been working on trying to find all the missing people from Windy Ridge—we even assembled a little task force to do just that."

"A feckin' task force?"

I nodded and motioned to Bud, Ol' Ned, Boone, and, after a moment, Dean. "That's actually why we came after your little... friend, there." My eyes fell on the shifter, who made an odd grunting noise in reply.

"Yeah, you got you some explainin' to do, Jim," Bud said.

Dean nodded, accepting the mug of hot moonshine (the only way Slim Jim liked to drink it) before sitting forward. Slim Jim, who'd dragged the single dining chair over to join us, looked at me in confusion.

"Who you talkin' 'bout?"

I pointed at the shifter in the cage. "Him."

Slim Jim turned around to get a good look at the hog-man. "Oh, him." Then he took a long sip of his drink. "That ain't no feckin' friend o' mine.'"

"Right well... whatever he is—he's been terrorizing Windy Ridge and he nearly killed one of our younger members," I finished, not hiding the bitterness in my voice.

"Yeah, that sounds about feckin' right."

I frowned at Slim Jim. "What do you mean that sounds right?"

Slim Jim looked at me and breathed out real slow and deliberate like. "When I said he weren't no friend o' mine what I meant was that he ain't no man."

"Well, what in tarnation is he then?" Ol' Ned asked.

Slim Jim motioned to the beast. "That there's a feckin' wild pig, born'n raised in these here feckin' woods."

We all paused.

Boone sat forward, setting his mug aside with a deeply furrowed brow. "W-w-what are you talkin' about, Jim?"

"Bud, you're a wolf man, right?" Slim Jim asked, brushing his long beard with one furry hand. Bud nodded. "An' me, I figured I'm some kinda feckin' were-beaver or somethin' like that."

"I thought you was a were muskrat," Bud said.

"Maybe, I don't feckin' know," Slim Jim answered on a shrug. "Point is—if you had t' guess what that feckin' thing is," he pointed to the shifter, "what would you say?"

"Uh…" Bud scratched the fur around his collar and I hoped he wasn't dropping fleas all over Slim Jim's house or I was fairly sure we weren't going to be invited back. "Um... a wereboar?"

"Wrong!" Slim Jim slapped his thigh and snapped. "That there's a feckin' *Boar-Were.*"

Something clicked in my head, and at the same time, Dean met my eyes, both of us staring at each other in shocked realization. Bud and Ol' Ned just looked confused, with the latter shoving the mug of hot moonshine onto the coffee table grumpily. "What in the heat o' hell are you talkin' about, Brother Jim?"

Instead of waiting for Slim Jim, Dean sat forward. "The 'were' prefix in 'werewolf' translates to 'man'. But Jim is using it as a *suffix* instead."

"What you goin' on about, boy?" Ol' Ned demanded and frustrated, I interrupted.

"This isn't a man that got turned into a boar," I explained, still in disbelief at what I was saying. "Slim Jim's saying this is a boar that got turned into a *man.*"

Bud and Ol' Ned were shocked silent, eyes wide and jaws hanging open. Boone looked the same as Boone always looked and Slim Jim just sat in his chair and sipped his cup with a smile.

"I call him Sonny."

"Sonny?" I repeated, thinking it an odd name for a horrible creature.

Slim Jim nodded. "Short for 'Sonova bitch'." Okay, that was more fitting. Slim Jim faced Dean then. "Sure am sorry he got to yer feller like that, Mr. Sheriff. He's a right bastard, kept feckin' sneakin' in here, tryin' ta eat all my vegee-ta-bles." Then he breathed out real hard and looked over at the hog-man. "Kinda fond of the little mess, though."

"Wait a second, wait just a darned second." Ol' Ned sat up straight and scooted his chair in Slim Jim's direction, his face shifting from frustration to intrigue as he faced me. "Twila, are you tellin' me humans ain't the only one's affected by the fog?"

"Right," I answered as I looked at Slim Jim. "At least, that's what I think Jim was trying to tell us."

"Sure feckin' am," Slim Jim replied.

"Sweet molasses," Ol' Ned said on an exhale.

"I been out here catchin' the stinkin' animals wanderin' 'round with their new human legs for months," Slim Jim continued. "In the back'a this property I made a place for some'a the more sane ones. Been teachin' 'em ta talk'n stuff."

"They can *talk?*" I asked, unable to hide the shock in my tone.

"Well, now, I didn't feckin' say *that.*" Slim Jim combed through his beard with a small grimace. "I said I been *teachin'* 'em to talk, but some of 'em ain't too bright."

"Can any of them talk?" Dean asked.

"Well, no," Slim Jim answered. "But there's this one were-squirrel that's lookin' to be promisin'."

"Summa bitch," Bud whispered as Ol' Ned gave Slim Jim a gummy smile and then slapped him on the shoulders.

"What other stuff've you done'n put around this little place o' yours, Brother Jim?"

Slim Jim smiled proudly and nodded to the western wall, where a fuse box looking device hung. "Infrared sensor. 'S how I knew Miss Twila was comin'. I use it ta make sure no dangerous feckin' critters come callin'."

"Infrared." Ol' Ned whispered in a low voice, and turned to Bud and Boone with a look of excitement. "We been thinkin'a fiddlin' with that for a while, haven't we, boys?"

Slim Jim paused, and then he began to smirk. "I like where this conversatin' is goin'."

Ol' Ned's interest spread onto the faces of Boone and Bud, and quietly, I let out a soft groan. Dean put his hand on my shoulder and leaned to whisper in my ear. "Are you alright?"

"I won't be," I mumbled. "'Cause when those damned hillbillies get ideas, somehow I always get sucked in."

I rubbed my eyes and watched Ol' Ned, Bud, and Boone gather around Slim Jim's chair, looking as picture-perfect as crazy friends could be. Bud slapped his paw onto Slim Jim's shoulder and grinned, lip curling with sharp canine teeth.

"Jim," he said, "how you like to join a hillbilly monster huntin' gang?"

Chapter Twenty
One Week Later

It took some talking to get Slim Jim to want to reintegrate into society, and honestly, I couldn't blame him.

He had it pretty good in his solitary shack out in the middle of nowhere, but eventually he conceded that he had grown a little lonely and the life of a hillbilly monster hunter would be a lot more fun, especially with his friends.

The boys decided to build a zoo of sorts beside Slim Jim's house where they could keep the various animal-turned-human shifters out of trouble. And it turned out Slim Jim had quite a few of them.

When we got back to Windy Ridge (courtesy of Ol' Ned who drove us), Dean asked if we could be dropped off at the Spider House to collect Mason.

Of course, Ol' Ned had obliged and I'd decided to go along with Dean because I wanted to make sure Mason was okay.

When we walked in, Edna was a little taken aback to see the very human sheriff but once we explained he was in the know, she calmed down. Then she explained that Mason was a very good patient and that Sicily had stayed with him the whole time during his ordeal. Dean grinned at me when Edna said as much and once again, I had to swallow down my motherly instinct to give that boy a talking-to right then. I just didn't know how I felt about Sicily dating and before Mason had walked into her life, dating hadn't even been on her radar, or on mine. Yep, the Hawkes were definitely uprooting our lives and I wasn't sure how to feel about it.

Regardless, Slim Jim received a warm welcome when he returned to town. The townsfolk were so surprised to see him that some of them began to plan a celebration, both for his return and the end to the boar-man attacks. Slim Jim didn't seem to care much for the people's excitement and instead, elected to spend the last few days in his cabin gathering his things, discussing tech with Ol' Ned and having Bud and Boone help him move his belongings back to his old trailer at River's Edge. As much of a headache as they were gonna be in the next few months, I was very happy to see my boys together again. Every time I passed by Ol' Ned's trailer in the days that followed, I could hear shouts and laughter, and I couldn't help but smile to myself.

Like a fool, however, I'd expected the next few

days to be far more peaceful than those before. The town was thrown into a bit of a roil as everyone rushed around to prepare for the 'Slim Jim welcome back party', but one pair of folks who didn't seem pleased were, of course, the Dooleys.

I received a knock on my door one evening when Dean and Mason were over for dinner. Cocking a brow at Sicily as if to ask 'who in the world could that be?', she peeked through the blinds, winced and turned slowly back to the dinner table.

"Thaaat's the mayor," she said, "and his wife, too. An' they don't look very happy."

"Oh, Lord." I put my head in my hands and sighed. "I knew Karen Dooley was gonna come back to bite me in the long run."

"The mayor?" Dean repeated. I glanced at him and saw him stone-faced, casting a rather serious look at the door.

I stood up then and walked over to the door, making sure Dean wasn't visible as I opened it. The last thing I wanted was for Karen Dooley to start giving him a hard time on account of me. Mayor Dooley, still chubby and furry even in his human form, was almost as red in the face as Karen, who was giving me the most disgustingly smug smile from over her husband's shoulder.

"Twila Boseman. I'm glad you're finally finished *running* from what you've done!" Said Mayor Dooley, looking every bit like the disgruntled rodent he was.

I cocked a brow at him. "Is that what I was doing?"

"Don't play *stupid,* you harlot," Karen hissed. "Dustin, arrest her for assault and battery. And kidnapping! And the obstruction of justice! Arrest her for all three an' for whatever else she's done that I ain't bringin' to mind at the moment!"

"Twila, you are under arrest," the mayor said calmly.

"For what?" I asked with a smirk.

"Well... you know what for."

"Remind me."

"Why... why you broke into our home and you trapped both my wife and me. And, of course, that's illegal!"

"Is it?"

"Well... yes! What you did cannot stand in the eyes of the law!" Mayor Dooley huffed and then reached for my wrist, as if he thought he could hold my hand and lead me to... well, wherever he planned on leading me. As far as I knew, he wasn't in the know about Dean being in the know about us. Before he could touch me though, I yanked my hand back, trying to repress a smirk of amusement.

"I seem to remember events differently," I said.

"How's that?" the mayor asked.

"From what I recall, you and your wife were plannin' on endangering the entire population of this town." I leaned against the door and shook my head. "Mayor, you know I would never have allowed that. Anyone in town you ask would agree with me. You and your wife were a danger to the rest of us, and I wasn't gonna let you risk everyone's lives so I simply did what I had to do."

"Well, now you're gonna answer for what you did."

"And how's that?" I continued. "Where are you plannin' on taking me?"

"Why, to the sheriff, of course." Hmm, so maybe he *was* in the know about Dean. "And once I explain to the sheriff what you did, why he'll throw you in a jail cell where you belong!"

"Will he?" I stepped back and glanced to the side. "Hey, Sheriff, are you plannin' on arrestin' me after hearin' that sob story?"

The Dooley's mouths fell open in unison as Dean sauntered into view, taking a moment to observe them before speaking.

"Arrest you?" He asked, folding his arms. "What for?"

"For assault, kidnapping and I forget what the third offense was," I answered.

"Battery!" Karen yelled out.

"Isn't that the same as assault?" I asked.

"Hmm." Dean rubbed his chin, and I could tell he was hiding a smirk under his hand. "It sounds to me like you were just trying to keep the town safe, Twila."

Karen grabbed her husband by the elbow and yanked him to the side. *"What?!* She *tied me up* inside my own home and with my own Christmas decorations! She threw him" (she then motioned to her insipid husband with a long, clawed black fingernail) "into a hamster cage!"

"And from what I recall, he enjoyed his time on his wheel quite a bit," I added and Dean had to forcibly hide his laugh behind clearing his throat.

"To stop the two of you from possibly endangering a society of people?" Dean shrugged. "As I see it, Twila just did what she had to do. If word got out to the rest of the world about you folks, you'd be in serious trouble. This is just simply a case of self-defense."

Then before they could say anything more and further upset my good evening, I gave the Dooleys a fluttering wave and slammed the door in their sputtering faces.

Then I gave Dean the same secretive smile he gave me and together, we walked back to the dinner table. I saw his eyes flick to mine and I grinned broadly at him as we settled down to finish our meal.

***

The dinner in honor of Slim Jim's return was hosted by the Damnation Diner. Dorcas was happy for the business, considering Sonny had cost her a lot. We conveniently left out the fact that Sonny was technically Slim Jim's pet...

Regardless, the smells of breakfast and greasy lunch foods filled the air as the residents of Windy Ridge welcomed back one of their own, as well as their freedom. A few days back, we'd dropped off letters to every household, filling the residents in about Dean and Mason. So, the celebration for Slim Jim also doubled as a coming out party or a rejoining society party for all those who had been in hiding since the sheriff had arrived.

Slim Jim, Bud, Boone, and Ol' Ned had gathered together in their own booth, seemingly challenging themselves to eat more than Sonny had when he broke in. Sicily walked in with Mason, who was on crutches, a short while later and I seated them in their own booth by the corner. But that was the extent of my working tonight—I was off the clock and I intended to remain that way. Pretty soon, I realized the whole place was packed but I managed to spot the only empty seat at the bar.

"Is this seat taken?" I asked Dean as I walked over, and he laughed, taking his coat off the stool and gesturing to it.

"I was saving it for you."

I sat down as I thanked him and watched Dorcas busily shout at the customers. She hadn't seen me come in which was just as well because I had a hunch she'd try to talk me into working. Not that I'd agree—as far as I was concerned, tonight was for enjoying and Dorcas and Hannah had everything under control.

"You look nice," Dean said as he turned to face me.

In honor of the special occasion, I'd put on something slightly more festive than my pink diner uniform, though it wasn't anything more than a halter top and a skirt. Still, I smiled to him and waved to his own outfit in reply.

"Look who's talking. I didn't know you owned a suit."

"Yeah, I'm not really a suit sort of guy," he sighed, and we both laughed as the diner atmosphere swelled around us. "I guess this is your prize."

"My prize?"

He nodded and gave me that sinner's smile of his. "Yeah. For winning the race. I said I'd take you to dinner."

I scoffed, tossing him a look. "Oh, you aren't getting off that cheap," I laughed.

"I was hoping you'd say that."

I gave him a raised brow expression. "Besides, I cheated."

"You did?" Dean blinked. "How?"

"If I was human, you would have whooped my butt." I rested my hand on my chin and sighed. "You didn't know I had, uh, *performance enhancers.*"

Dean laughed again, but once he looked at me, the laugh died in his throat and his brows softened just a hint. "Well, I'll keep your secret, Twila Boseman."

My smile widened. Everything felt warm when he looked at me that way, an odd bout of safety resting in my chest that I hadn't felt in a long time. "You know," I said, "I never thought I'd say this, but I should go thank Karen sometime."

"Thank Karen?" he frowned.

I nodded. "Yeah. The only reason I purposely sought you out was because she decided to endanger this whole town by meeting with you."

Dean turned and gently took my hands. He looked handsome and calm and those eyes—yes, they brought me back all those years all over again.

"Well, I think you need to refigure that story," he whispered as he leaned in.

"Refigure what story?"

"The reason why you sought me out," he answered and he was so close, I could have sworn he was going to kiss me.

"And what should I refigure it to?"

He shrugged. "How about that an old flame walked into your life after twenty-three years and you decided to pick up right where you left off?"

I smiled and then cocked my head to the side, pretending to think on it. "And this flame?"

"Yes?"

"Did he feel the same way about me?"

He hummed and put his hand on my face and then he brought me in close, warm hands on warm skin, and I melted towards him, listening to the party going on around me, but not really hearing it.

Dean chuckled. "He sure did. Still does.""

The End

Return to Trailer Park!
Hillbillies and HellHounds
Trailer Park Vampire #2
by J.R. Rain and H.P. Mallory
Coming soon!

We hope you enjoyed *Shotguns and Shifters*! If so, please help spread the word by leaving a review! Thank you!

About J.R. Rain

J.R. Rain is the international bestselling author of over seventy novels, including his popular Samantha Moon and Jim Knighthorse series. His books are published in five languages in twelve countries, and he has sold more than 3 million copies worldwide.

Please find him at: www.jrrain.com.

About H.P. Mallory

H.P. Mallory is a New York Times and USA Today bestselling author. She has eleven series currently and she writes paranormal fiction, heavy on the romance! H.P. lives in Southern California with her son and a cranky cat.

To learn more about H.P. and to download free books, visit: www.hpmallory.com

Made in the USA
Monee, IL
26 November 2022